Transitions and

Awakenings:

No Regrets

Transitions and Awakenings: No Regrets

With stories by:

Laura Hardgrave

R. J. Joseph

David Rheinhart

Sierra July

Jason Kimble

Anton Rose

James Beamon

K.B. Spangler

Robin M Black

Carlos Hernandez

Edited by:

Ereika Collins

Sanguine Press

Sanguine Press

TRANSITIONS AND AWAKENINGS:
NO REGRETS

PRINT ISBN: 978-0-9981769-0-1
EBOOK ISBN: 978-0-9981769-1-8

www.Sanguine.press

A blessing and dedication:
May your imagination bring you
light in times of darkness.

Table of Contents

Technically Magic
by Jason Kimble

Brody was deep in the middle of a South Dakota blizzard, maxing the heat generator on the classic 2065 Hovington Flicker when he felt his mana surge. He uncoupled his cyberlink and disengaged acceleration before the surge hit, but he was still heading for the ground at 100 mph when the inertial safeties shut down in response to physics going sideways.

Brody sucked in his breath and scrambled to find something useful in the rune field he'd spontaneously generated.

"Come on ... no, not speed ... no, we're *avoiding* pain, thanks... oh for the love of ... really, *acid?* Ah!"

He snatched a pentagonal protective rune with his organic right hand and threw it for the front of the vehicle. Backhanded the concentric icons of expansion after it. As he was pinching the curlicues of softening, he missed the dissolution rune. It hit his shoulder. He felt the null ward tear open between the nanotech interface at the top of his cybernetic left arm and the nerves at his shoulder joint. The Flicker landed without a scratch, but the pain as Brody's internal electromagnetic and mana fields commingled left him wishing for a collision.

Brody ignored the sparks as stray runes hit the Flicker's control panel. He was busy pulling at the torn edges of the ward. He pinched his organic thumb and two middle fingers together to manifest the proper restoration rune. Biting down on a scream, he slipped the rune into his shoulder, then gasped as the pain fell away. The cybernetic joints in his left hand relaxed out of the spasm a cascading failure had started.

Finally able to notice something other than the nihilistic war of one section of his body against the other, Brody swore. Climate controls were mana-fried, and the nothing response he got trying to initiate liftoff meant both mag-lev and cyclones were offline. In fact, when he was done swearing, about the only sound left in the car was the howling blizzard.

"Fuck," he moaned.

Now he was done swearing.

Brody thought about runing up heat against the screaming, sideways snow, but before he used any more mana, he wanted to know how he'd gotten full enough to surge. Brody switched off his right eye and set his link nodes to a sleep cycle. The cyber tech in his head effectively dormant, he could access his channel senses again.

"Holy..."

There wasn't a direction he looked that wasn't saturated. He hadn't seen this much pure, untapped mana in ... that would be never. He was vaguely surprised he'd gotten as far as he had before his cells couldn't hold any more.

Runing heat wouldn't be a problem when he needed it, at least. But creating the ambient field would hose his uplink, so heat later. Brody closed his senses off and brought his implants back online.

There might not be much civilization out this far, but at least the signal was strong.

Kota Driveaway Service. Connecting to...?

Brody bounced Rashmi's code to the server.

Connection protocol?

Brody requested VAI. He didn't need a digitally-constructed environment to translate beam interactions for him, but Brody wanted the ego soothing. He glanced at his avatar in the simulated office's mirror. In the cold car, he was a hot mess. With two twitches of the signal, here his ginger beard and hair were trimmed and styled. He even had on his favorite shirt, the one that showed off all the chest and bicep work he'd been doing.

Vain, but he figured he deserved it after the touchdown. He didn't imagine Rashmi was walking around clean and fresh, skin burnished to perfection, and fully dressed at two in the morning, either, so it wasn't like the nudging of self-image didn't go both ways.

"You're on time and there are no problems and you just wanted to call and tell me how perfect this gig's going, right, Kerr?" Rashmi asked, sarcasm practically visible in her code.

"There was a little--"

"Client's expecting his car in three days. You were already running behind."

"I can catch up," Brody said. "We landed gold, but I had a mana surge. Flicker needs some circuit replacements. Probably a reboot."

"Why the hell didn't you flush beforehand?" Rashmi asked, throwing her virtual hands in the air. Brody crossed his own in front of his chest.

"Rashmi. I flushed my mana store. This route, though. If there was a way to transmit mana density, you'd see this place is like the Grand Canyon of mana."

"What the hell good is magic if you can't see the future?" Rashmi asked.

Brody was tempted, not for the first time, to break down the tangled mess magic became when temporality got involved. But one of the first things Brody learned when he opened was that the twisted logic of magic only sticks in your brain when you use it. Resourceful as Rashmi was, she was still mundane.

"The point is," he said instead, "I ran smack into what amounts to a mana flood, and since I was plugged in--"

"Yeah, yeah. Cyber-link turns off your juju senses," Rashmi said, holding up her hand. She pinched her nose just beneath her bindi, breathed in once, then looked back up.

"Let me call up ... " her avatar froze and flickered a moment. "I've got a repair scheduled with an outfit in Canton. Looks like that's the closest town."

"How long?"

Rashmi glanced up at the order Brody couldn't see. "At least two hours for pickup. They have to recall a crew to get a retrieval on site. Apparently, they also run the internal city path maintenance and, you know: blizzard."

"Don't worry. I'll make arrangements for myself," Brody said, smirking.

Rashmi rolled her avatar's eyes. "Just set the beacon and do ..." Rashmi waved her hands and closed her virtual eyes, "... whatever you're gonna do. Just promise not to make trouble," Rashmi warned.

"Rashmi..."

She raised a digital eyebrow, and Brody laughed.

"I promise." he said.

"This is coming out of your fees," Rashmi added, then cut the link.

"You're a sweetheart, Rashmi."

Blizzard temps were seeping past the Flicker's hearty insulation. Time for those other arrangements. Brody matched the curves of a calling glyph with twinned runes for sympathy, then popped them onto the waveform for imagery.

"You're kidding," he muttered, studying the faintly glowing seeming. "Only one within fifty miles? What kind of backwater is this?"

At least the one was cute. Square jaw. Dark, smooth skin. Brody did like the look of those broad shoulders. What the hell. Brody tapped the calling rune.

He waited all of fifteen seconds. Seemed Brody wasn't the only person desperate for a ride.

#

Micah was an even more imposing wall of muscle in person. Not that Brody was complaining. Brody was swearing a lot again, but this time it was all the good kind. Lasted longer, too.

"I didn't think they did cybernetic augments on channels," Micah asked as they lay in the rumple of sheets afterward. Brody sighed. He was a talker. Brody rolled onto his side, pushed the shock of ginger out of his own eyes, and smirked.

"When they know you're a channel, they don't," Brody said. "But my parents are mundane, and I was born a little ... incomplete?" he said.

"I'm sorry," Micah said, cringing visibly. Brody shrugged.

"They're good augments," he said. "Scaling nanotech, easy-upgrade beaming links. I can't complain. Well, I complained a lot the day I opened, of course ...."

Brody rolled onto his back again to avoid the pity in Micah's deep brown eyes. Shoved aside the memory of the first time his body tried to tear itself apart. He held up the cybernetic arm, looked at it instead of Micah.

"Took half a dozen specialists to build the warding," he said. "Luckily, the folks were loaded and there's only the one of me."

Brody shook it off and sat up.

"Your turn," Brody said as he propped himself up with his organic arm.

"I don't have any augments," Micah said with an open smile. Good, the pity was gone.

"No: life share for life share," Brody said. "You are the only channel on the espernet in a ridiculous spread of space."

"I feel so special you chose me from all your options, then," Micah snarked back. Brody cocked his head to the side and raised an eyebrow.

"I grew up here," Micah said, sitting up himself.

"Doesn't explain why you're still in mundane-istan."

"My sister," Micah said.

Brody had to lunge back to avoid catching his left arm chassis in the cloud of recall and imagery runes Micah tossed out. In the seeming, Micah's sister looked like a sweet enough kid. The same deep brown skin as Micah. Big, brown eyes, too. Overgrown cloud of tight, black curls.

"Hannah. It started when she was 10," Micah said. Definitely a talker. He couldn't just give the facts, he had to spin the Epic Origin Tale. Wired guys never had this problem. What he wouldn't give for a databeam transfer to speed things along.

The image widened as the little girl threw off an impressive mana surge. Papers and books and even a small chair got caught up in the spinning energy as Hannah bent the laws of nature for the first time. From the stuffed unicorn in the debris, Brody figured it was her room. Two adults and a skinny, teenaged boy shielded their eyes and clung to each other in the doorway.

"That's you?" Brody asked, pointing with his organic side. He glanced over to real-Micah and gave him a wink. "You filled out well."

Micah chuckled, cheeks going slightly darker as he blushed.

"Thanks," he said, but pushed on. "When Hannah opened, she opened me, too." The adults screamed and ran for cover as the storm threw several runes into young Micah. His eyes flared green, and a second surge fed into the first. The picture window off to one side shattered under the barrage of force and fragility iconography Micah manifested, glass mixing with the rest of the debris and randomized runes.

"Not the kind of two-fer a guy's usually after," Brody quipped, nudging Micah's bare shoulder with his own. Another rune flicked at the seeming, shifting the scene.

"We don't .... Canton's not exactly channel-friendly," Micah said while Brody saw some kind of rally. A dark olive-skinned woman in a sharp business suit, her hair pulled back tight into a sleek ponytail, stood behind a podium. She spoke to a crowd who waved signs with winning phrases like *No Devil 4 Our Kidz* and *Clear The Taint*.

"Yeah," Brody said. "Getting that. She is?"

"Lila Castillo. That pain you told me you get when your wards fail? Castillo made something that does it on purpose."

"You're shitting me."

Micah shook his head and flicked another rune. Hannah was now being fitted with some sort of torque.

"Monitors the body for signs of mana build up, then releases nanotech when you have enough to rune." Within the seeming, Hannah jerked tense as lights on the torque flashed red. Eyes closed tight, jaw clenched, she scratched an emptying rune in the air. There was a soft glow, then the lights on the torque turned green and Hannah relaxed.

"Only way to stop it is to flush," Brody said. Micah nodded.

"Theory is, if you flush enough without manifesting anything else, the body stops soaking mana."

"They know it doesn't work that way, right?" Brody said.

Micah shrugged. "Castillo's labs swear by their research models."

Brody sighed. "*Scientific* research models?"

Micah nodded.

"Seriously? Even out here they have to know mana breaks every rule--"

"--but its own," Micah finished, falling back onto the pillows. Brody lay back with him.

"So ... how come you don't have a flushy collar thing?"

"I was eighteen by then. Laws around here aren't friendly to channels, but they still need consent to perform medical treatments."

"That's not medicine."

"They only needed *parental* consent for Hannah." Micah's voice grew tight. He threw a jagged dismissal at the seeming and rolled away from Brody. The image of Hannah's tear-streaked face broke apart and dissolved back into the mana field.

You promised not to make trouble, Brody thought, staring at Micah's back: solid, broad, and quivering just a bit. Brody didn't need to see his face to know it was as wet as Hannah's in the seeming.

A promise is a promise, he thought. This was just a hookup. Two people helping each other forget how messed up life was. Brody lay his hand on Micah's shoulder. Kissed the back of his neck.

Micah rolled back to Brody at the contact, buried his face in the divot where Brody's neck met his chest. He hugged Brody close. The same muscles that had been supple and responsive earlier clung to Brody like he was the only thing keeping Micah afloat.

#

Brody slipped out of the rumpled bed and into a chair at Micah's small kitchen table the next morning. Last time he slept so poorly was from curling up in the back of a compact Flystorm in the middle of Iowa. He scratched at his beard, then tapped his temple with cybernetic fingers to beam the coffeemaker on. He sketched matching memory and imagery runes with his other hand.

Hannah's surge flared to life in a new seeming. It really *was* an impressive primary surge. The environmental runes weren't surprising. So many of them working in concert, though. He flicked a focus rune and zoomed in on Hannah.

Three kinds of ward runes spontaneously. Gravity and stabilizing runes keeping her floating dead center of the storm while she struggled to pull it all back. None of it on its own was out of the ordinary, but all stacked up like that? What this girl's potential must be. Where she would be if she hadn't spent six years locked down by some technically-legal torture device.

This runing was crazy. There was one on her forearm that almost tickled Brody's senses *through* the seeming.

"I smell coffee," Micah called from the bedroom. Brody tossed a dissolution at the seeming.

Micah was rubbing sleep from his eyes, leaning against the aluminum headboard when Brody came in with two mugs. Micah stretch-yawned. Brody could swear he'd placed the sheet strategically to show off everything but the business.

"Thank god," Micah said as he sat up straight to take his mug. He sipped the coffee, made a noise somewhere close to a purr, then leaned back on the headboard, eyes closed. "You're a prince."

"A count, maybe," Brody said, sitting on the edge of the bed. "A prince would have made breakfast."

"Point," Micah said. He smiled, then it fell into a sheepish stare into his mug. "I'm … sorry I unloaded on you last night," he muttered.

"Really?" Brody said with a crooked smile. "It's not like I didn't return the sticky favor."

Micah gave Brody's organic arm a playful backhanding. "You know what I mean," he said.

Brody bit his lip. It was his turn to stare into a mug. "Yeah. I mean, no, it's okay, and I was thinking..."

Promise not to make trouble, Rashmi's voice chided in his head.

"Oh?" Micah said.

A promise is a promise, came his own thoughts from the night before.

Brody looked back up, to Micah and his worried puppy expression.

A promise is a rule, Brody decided, *and mana breaks every rule but its own.*

"The Flicker seats four. Not a lot of room for luggage, but ought to be enough if no one minds being snug."

"You're ... asking me to run away with you?" Micah asked.

"No," Brody said, "I'm asking you to run away with your sister."

#

Brody let out another swearing streak as the null ward imploded for the he-couldn't-even-keep-track time.

"That *hurts!*" Hannah snapped as she pulled another emptying rune from the air to cancel out the torque's painful feedback. "Are you sure he even knows what he's doing?"

Hannah had grown up since the image in Micah's seeming. Her do wasn't quite as severe as Micah's buzz cut, but the wild cloud of tight curls wasn't nearly as large as it had been on ten-year-old Hannah. Late teens Hannah had a sense of style to her. Pity she had to accessorize everything around the cattle prod on her neck.

"*He* is right here. And not deaf," Brody said. The three of them sat around Micah's kitchen table in the late day light. Brody was trying to replicate his shoulder's null ward to circumvent the tech linked into Hannah. For the fifth consecutive hour.

"Not an answer," Hannah shot back, crossing her arms.

"He's trying to help," Micah assured her, then turned to Brody. "She's under a lot of stress."

"She's sixteen," Brody said, as if that explained everything. It at least explained how the girl slipped out of the house to meet her pariah brother on an hour's notice. Brody recalled having at least half a dozen good escape routes and excuses when he was her age for when boys, trouble, or--when he was really lucky--both called.

"Still not hearing an answer," Hannah said.

Micah bit his lip and looked to Brody. "*Are* you sure you can do this?"

"I don't know any more," Brody said, flopping back in his chair and turning the seeming of his own ward around in the air next to him.

"I've been dealing with this--" he gestured with both his cybernetic and organic hands to the complex interlacing of runes--"for long enough to do my own regular patch work on the warding. I'm intimately aware of where the ouches happen. But I'm not a chirurgeon or a cyber-tech. Definitely not the kind my parents' money bought to design this thing in the first place."

"Seriously with this guy?" Hannah said.

"Everybody breathe," Micah said before Brody could snap back. He put a hand on each of their shoulders. It was dangerous how quickly that contact rocketed Brody's endorphin levels. A glance to Hannah proved her own tensions softened, as well.

"You were close that time," Micah said. "It looked almost like the model."

"He's right," Hannah piped in, though Brody hadn't missed the small squeeze of Micah's hand on her shoulder to prompt it.

"It's the null rune," Brody said, flicking the seeming to float between the three of them. He pointed to the stretched and extended runing along one side.

"The *point* of a null rune is to shut down active energies it touches," Brody said as much to himself as the others. "Grafting one onto runing we want to perpetuate is ... "

"Counter-intuitive," Micah said. Brody nodded. The three of them sat in silence a moment, the seeming slowly spinning on an unseen axis.

"Stop it a second," Hannah said. She couldn't actually make contact with it for fear she'd soak some portion of the mana.

"What do you see?" Micah asked, grabbing the seeming and holding it still.

"Nothing, but I was thinking ... can you make this bigger?" she asked.

Brody nodded. "Move back."

Hannah backpedaled as Brody slung an expansion rune into the seeming. The image blew up until it was tall enough to bump ceiling and floor. At that size, they all saw it. There, at the point where delicate runic stitching connected the stretched null rune to the rest of the matrix.

"An inversion rune," Hannah said, eyes bright.

"Un-nulls the null," Brody muttered, brows furrowing as he watched mana twist in on itself at the junction.

"And the null undoes the inversion," Hannah added. "So it can still block the rest of the mana."

"How is that again?" Micah asked, crossing his arms and squinting at the same spot.

"Stop trying to use mundane logic on it," Brody said. "Breaks every rule, remember?" He'd mucked about with his ward so many times before, and not only hadn't he noticed the inversion, it would never have occurred to him to look. Brody bit the inside of his cheek and studied Hannah a minute as she stood, arms crossed and head cocked.

"Now we try again, right?" Hannah asked with a smile.

"Tomorrow," Brody said. "I'm wiped, and even with the missing piece, this is going to take a while. Better to do it fresh."

Hannah shot Micah wide, pleading eyes.

"The Flicker won't be ready until tomorrow," Brody added before Micah could use the same trick on him. "Without that, we're still stuck here and that thing's still stuck on Hannah's neck."

The siblings' shoulders both sagged, but they relented.

#

Brody was up half the night, but once he knew what he was looking for, things started falling into place. He had the ward ready by the next afternoon, just around the time Rashmi pinged that the Flicker was hale and hearty.

Brody took a deep breath, held it, then phased the ward in along the torque's interface nodes. He cycled the cybernetics in his head back online and shifted his right eye's input spectrum to check the nanobinders under Hannah's skin.

"Is that it?" Micah asked softly.

"Yeah," Brody said. "I think so."

"How do we know it worked?" Hannah whispered, holding herself like the slightest move could set something off.

"Try to manifest a rune," Brody said. "If the light turns red, we know I'm still a screw-up."

Hannah broke her statue impression to give Micah an incredulous look.

"Please tell me he was at least really good in bed," Hannah said.

Micah's cheeks darkened as he studied the table. Hannah giggled.

The giggle fell away as she took a deep breath, then held a finger up and sketched a light rune in the air. It melted into an orange, glowing sphere that hung in the air, but the LED on the torque stayed green.

That was the end of stillness. Micah jumped out of his chair, knocking it to the ground with a loud bang. He swept Hannah up in a bear hug, spun her in a circle as she laughed. It was bright and hopeful and infectious, and Brody's cheeks were sore from how wide he was smiling by the time Micah let his sister's feet touch the floor again.

Brody walked over and pressed the Flicker's validation fob into Micah's palm.

"I'm wiped," he said. "She's wiped. Can you pick up the car while we take half a second to breathe?"

Micah kissed Brody by way of answer. It was short and reassuring and only briefly reminded him of their far less chaste evenings prior.

When Micah was gone, Hannah cocked her head and crossed her arms. No warm up, then. Brody shrugged.

"I thought alone time would be good," Brody said.

Hannah raised an eyebrow but didn't say anything. Brody was uncomfortably reminded of Rashmi. She was going to kill him for this.

Which was why he needed to know exactly how deep this hole went.

"Your brother built a seeming when he told me about your problem," Brody said. "Hell of a show you put on when you opened," he added, quick-sketching a pair of runes. The seeming from the other night returned. Hannah looked away.

"I don't like remembering," she muttered. "They were all so afraid of me. And then Micah ... "

"That's pretty common," Brody said. He gestured to the mana-fueled storm Hannah wasn't looking at. "Basic infusion. Maybe it temporarily animates a chair, maybe someone with latent talent like your brother winds up opened. You usually get a mix of basic energetic runes, too, like the cyclones and lightings here." Brody gestured, pointing to the scattered spiral and jagged runes as he mentioned them.

"Instinctive self-warding runes, levitation. It's a lot, but I thought it was the massive pool around here. I didn't catch on at first."

Hannah glanced back to Brody, frowning.

"Didn't even fully catch on at second. Dismissed the whole idea as crazy. But then you lead us to the null-inversion gestalt in my ward."

"Just a good guess," Hannah said. Brody shook his head.

"You're a natural, but there's only so far raw talent gets you. Understanding the really twisty parts of magic? You only get there with practice. That leap you took meant my idea didn't seem quite so crazy. Took a page from you and decided a closer look might clear things up."

Brody jabbed his thumb to the seeming. A small rune froze the scene, then slowly zoomed the image in on Hannah's right wrist. Brody pointed to the vaguely eye shaped rune on her skin. Zoomed in this way, there was no mistaking the intricate internal patterns of it. Patterns that shifted as they watched, despite the fact the seeming was frozen.

"Prescience," Brody said.

"I don't know what you're--"

"Mana breaks all the rules, but time's a particularly tight knot to unravel. This isn't instinctive or primal. You only manifest one of these if you've been building it for a very long while."

They both watched the seeming a moment, silent.

"Six," Hannah finally said. "I was really six when I opened."

Brody didn't respond.

"I figured, if I hid it long enough, I could work out how to get rid of it. You've seen what they think about channels here. But the more I used it, the stronger it got. Then I managed a prescience rune."

Hannah shook her head. Her face broke with a wry smile.

"You thought that null inversion was compli-cated?" she said. "Try the mind-blower when dozens of probability trails hit at once. I saw a way through that would let me hide. Keep my head down, get out when I was old enough. Have a normal life, like any other playing-fair chan-nel."

Hannah's hand hovered in front of the cyber-netic torque, though she didn't touch it.

"But I saw this thing. Saw them test it on half a dozen low-rent channels. Perfect the tech, build the support base, and then boom! Kids locked down and zapped 'clean' every which way I looked. There was only one direction where Castillo's Electric People Collar wound up shut down, and it was by latching it around *my* neck."

"You let them do this to you?" Brody asked, incredulous. Hannah looked ahead, through the seeming not at it.

"I knew it would hurt," she said, "But if I worked it right? I was gonna hurt them a whole lot more. Channels have power, but they're all so worried about being nice and nonthreatening. Meanwhile, the mundanes are building this stuff." Hannah spread her hands beneath the torque, its green light on now that they'd fooled its sensors with the null ward.

"Problem was, once I put it on? I needed someone else to get it off."

Brody flinched.

"You opened Micah on purpose," Brody said.

"I couldn't get out of here alone," Hannah said. "Not after they shackled me. And Micah would have been sad, but you just said it: you can't truly understand magic unless you live it."

"And I wouldn't find him if he didn't open first," Brody tried. Hannah shrugged, then finally met Brody's eyes again.

"You won't tell him," Hannah said flatly.

Brody only raised an eyebrow in response.

"You and I know there's no closing a channel once it's open," Hannah said, holding Brody's eyes with her own. "But we're never going to convince Castillo and her bat shit crazy torture team of that. That only stops with the right martyrs: the tortured innocent and her loyal, long-suffering brother. The world needs the rallying point. Micah's going to need someone to help him weather the circus this is going to be, but the other thing you and I both know is that isn't going to be you."

Hannah stopped and raised her own eyebrow. Brody bit the inside of his cheek but didn't say anything.

"There's a reason you picked a job where you're never in one place for too long."

The Flicker's proximity sensor pinged Brody. Micah was waiting.

"He deserves better," Brody muttered as he picked up his bag.

"Most people do," Hannah said, grabbing her own and Micah's.

Micah sat at the controls when they got outside. Six years of fear and isolation. Six years never quite giving up, but never quite having hope, either.

For Hannah it had been a decade.

Better, yes, but Brody wasn't sure he could come up with what that better might be.

There were no words or runes, but as Brody glanced to Hannah one more time, they signed an accord all the same.

Micah slid to the passenger seat as Brody took the controls, and the slightest bit of tension fell out of Brody's shoulders.

This was something he knew. How to push a hovercar fast and far enough until you don't have to think about where you used to be, and watch where you are fall away almost as quick.

The destination was already locked. The only thing left was to make the most out of the ride.

Brody coupled his cyberlink and punched the throttle.

END

Luz is the Light of My Life
by Carlos Hernandez

The white noise of Miami Beach nightlife helps camouflage my partner and me. Every night is Carnival here, with revelers--costumed, hypersexualized, stupefied by alcohol--risking everything to unmoor themselves from their lives of mundane woe. It's a Tuesday, so (thankfully) fewer people stumble along the sidewalks choosing which bar to patronize next.

We're walking to "Clean, Well-Lighted," a restaurant that used to be cool. I am wearing a dress the case profiler called "classy," "age-appropriate," "dowdy, but in a good way." The only time I ever wear dresses is in missions. And heels. These fucking heels.

Valentin is worse off. Poor bastard hasn't been suit-shopping in years; I'd bet a thousand dollars his mami bought this one for him before he got married. But Valentin has been working out since then. If he flexed the suit would explode and he'd be naked.

To keep the mood light--you keep the mood light or the disontological will wink you out--I tell him that.

"You'd like that, wouldn't you?" he replies. Then he stops and goes through a series of body-builder poses. He's joking, but he loves showing off his body. You can tell.

I roll my eyes and keep moving. He scrambles and catches up. "What's wrong, Doña Boss Lady?" he says. "Too much man for you?"

"Your zipper's down," I answer without looking.

He stops, checks; I laugh and pick up the

pace. When he catches up he says, not una-
mused, "If you cry wolf, next time I won't believe
you."

"Just keep your wolf in your pants, or I really
will cry."

Not the best badinage in the world, I know.
But it does the job; Valentin laughs, and then I
kind of do, too. I can't convince myself not to be
scared out of my mind, but if I can convince Valentin, he might be able to save both our lives.
He's a new recruit, you see. He has no idea what
we're facing.

But I do. All too well. I could never take a target like Esmeralda Desasida into custody by myself because I know she's right and the rest of us
are wrong. The only genuine defense against di-
sontologicals is ignorance.

#

The cafe's dead-ahead, alfresco seating even
at this time of night. Esmeralda's alone in the

restaurant, drinking red wine by the carafe. She tips the rest of the wine into her glass, then holds the kicked carafe aloft, doesn't look backwards. Seconds later a waiter appears and puts a full one on the table and takes the empty out of her hand and hustles off like he knows what can happen if he gets on her bad side.

"¿That's her?" says Valentin. "¿That's the big threat?"

"Don't underestimate her."

"What's she going to do, take out her knitting needles? Tell us stories and bore us to death? Oh, I know--she'll give us some of that disgusting old-lady candy. That stuff will kill you."

I laugh. It's fake, but I'm a good actor. I can feel Valentin's pleasure. He thinks I think he's hilarious.

I saunter causally out of the alleyway, doing my best to look touristy and unaware. Valentin keeps up. As we walk I whisper, "Remember, she's suffering through a psychotic break. We need to bring her back to reality enough to take her into custody."

"Affirmative," he says.

I open the gate to the restaurant's outdoor seating and weave quickly through the tables and sit down at Esmeralda's. Valentin comes over and stands next to me.

Esmeralda turns slowly to look at me. Her face is somewhere between bemused and amused. "¿Aren't you a little old to be a whore?" she asks finally, in Spanish. Miami Spanish, just like mine. "Ah, but that would explain why you're so aggressive, sitting down at people's tables unbidden. ¿These days you have to fight to get your business, eh vieja? Well, bad luck for you, but I'm not a lesbian. And," she adds, glancing briefly at Valentin, "you couldn't pay me to sleep with him."

"That's right," says Valentin. "You couldn't."

I smile, weave my finger together on the table. In English: "I'm not a whore. But I did come here specifically to find you, Mrs. Desasida. And you didn't try to kill me right away. That's a good sign."

Her face drops. Her mouth is guilty, aggrieved. "You're here to arrest me."

Valentin says, "Wrong again. It's true that you're in trouble. But it's trouble your own mind is creating. We are here to help you."

She doesn't look at him. She's figured out I'm in charge. She picks up her wine and swirls it and doesn't drink. But she does take a histrionic whiff of it. More to her glass than to me she says, "Did I invent them?"

Before Esmeralda can erase me, I look at Valentin, who screws up his face as if to say, "¿Isn't it hilarious, how batshit crazy this woman is?"

I smile at him, then turn back to Esmeralda.

She's disappointed. "You're still here."

Valentin huffs. "Why would we leave?"

Esmeralda puts down the glass and leans in a little. "Okay. You have my attention. Who are you?"

I speak with the affectless lilt of a bureaucrat. "I am Doctor Xalvadora Chaviano Viejó, and this is Doctor Valentin Evora. We're from the United Nations Department of Psychiatric Interventions. As Dr. Evora said, we're here to help you."

Esmeralda's eyes are shrewd and small. "¿How stupid do you think I am?"

"We have credentials," says Valentin, then reaches into his coat pocket and throws a leather wallet on the table; it falls open near her, revealing his U.N. identification. On the other side of the wallet--God fucking damn it--is a picture of his wedding day, his vivacious bride, Luz, smiling next to him.

Personal effects like pictures are expressly

forbidden on subdue/eliminate missions for di-sontologicals. Valentin must have been told that a million times in training. But he's a newlywed, and newlyweds are idiots. I should have checked; this is my error as much as it is his. But there's nothing to do now but to pretend nothing's wrong.

"Ask your phone about us," Valentin says to Esmeralda. "You'll see everything's in order."

She does exactly that: she takes her phone out of her purse and takes a picture of the ID and taps the touchscreen a few times and waits for the results of her query to appear. They do; her eyes read; the touchscreen's light cast her face in blue-white light. Then she's done reading and she stows her phone in her purse and looks at me.

"If you're really from the U.N.," says Esmeralda, "then you know who I am. I expect to be treated with respect. Make sure your subordinate understands that."

Valentin crosses his arms like an angry djinn. "Respect? We're authorized by the United Nations to take you by force if we have to. Even kill you, if the situation merited it."

And I, as good cop: "Obviously, we'd prefer handling the situation in a much more respect-ful manner."

She smiles at me, leans back, drinks, drinks. "Why do I do this to myself?" she asks the night sky. "Why do I threaten to kill myself? I wonder if a gun my mind invented would actually kill me. Or would I just awake, the way you do when you die in dreams? Would Manuel bring me cafecito in bed like he used to and pet my hair and say 'It was just a nightmare, mi vida'?"

She dumps the rest of the wine into her mouth and says "¡Ah!" and then turns to me and says, "I'm too much of a coward to find out. I've disappeared your guns."

Valentin--fool!--pats himself down, and yes,

his gun is gone, and he makes a production of saying, "What? Where is my ... how did you ... Xalvadora, what the ...?" Every time he fails to complete a sentence he gives her power. I need him to shut up. Which means I need to produce our guns.

And so I look down to my purse, leaning against my right foot, to help me believe in my purse. It's a simple affair, strapless, soft black leather with a brass buckle that's a little too big and ostentatious for my taste. But that buckle is easy to remember, to recreate in my mind. I look at the purse and think *This is my purse* and every time I try to deny the purse--for it is our nature to deny the reality of the real--the purse asserts itself before my eyes and against my ankle.

From there, I imagine the interior of the purse. When I left for this mission I emptied it save for one item, a fully-loaded Sig Sauer P229. I have taken that gun apart and reassembled it so many times that I know it better than my own viscera. I have placed my trust in every spring and screw, and in the interlocking system they create for detonating a small, reliable explosion that will launch a conical projectile 1,350 feet per second from its muzzle and, assuming my aim is true, instantly dissolve the dasein of my target. *My gun is in my purse*, I think to myself.

I pick up the purse and place it on the table and look at Esmeralda who parries me smile for smile. I unbuckle the purse and pull out my pistol and place it on the table next to Valentin's ID.

"It will only fire for me, so don't get any ideas," I tell her. "But go ahead, pick it up." And then, since I think she will appreciate the irony, "Touch it and believe."

It's Esmeralda's turn to be disconcerted. She takes the gun, ponders its heft. Then she points it at me and strains to pull the trigger.

"I just told you it will only fire for me," I say.

She shrugs, puts the gun down where it was. "You could have been lying. Why could I make his gun disappear but not yours?"

"You didn't make his gun disappear. I did." Then I reach into my purse and pull out another Sig Sauer: one I have just now imagined into existence. I place it on the table next to mine.

Both Esmeralda and Valentin gasp. "But I had my gun as we were crossing the plaza," says Valentin. "I remember specifically putting my hand in my coat pocket to check on it. ¿When did you have the time--?"

"Not three minutes into our conversation with Mrs. Desasida you threatened to kill her if she doesn't cooperate. Is that how you were trained to behave?"

Shame rises red in Valentin's face. "I was only trying to--"

"I disarmed you before you could spark a tragedy and ruin your own life. It was a simple

thing to accomplish. You need to be more attentive."

"I am extremely attentive," says Esmeralda.
"And I did not see you reach into his coat pocket
and disarm him either."

"With all due respect, you are not capable of
being attentive right now, Mrs. Desasida. It is
difficult to say without a proper psychological
work-up, but you have given us much reason to
believe that you are in the midst of a psychotic
break. There may even be confabulation involved, though for that diagnosis we would need
to establish a physiological cause. The point is,
you need our help. I hope you see that. I hope
my little 'magic show' has proven to you that you
cannot make things disappear with a thought."

"¿Where is my husband, then?" Her bottom
teeth bite her upper lip. Her eyes zig-zag, scan-
ning the world for understanding. "Manuel. My
Manuel. I didn't mean to. I didn't know I could."

Valentin is about to interrupt her, but I grip his wrist. To counter her story, we needed the details. And she had been waiting for a long time for a confessor.

She falls back into her chair and speaks to the heavens. "It was a stupid fight. It was infuriating, fighting him, because he never raised his voice and insisted on being logical and conciliatory. When I fight, I rage and burn myself out; later I apologize. So I wished him dead and gone at one point. I meant it in the moment, I won't lie. But I didn't *really* mean it.

"But too late. My wish came true. He disappeared a dimension at a time, like the image on an old-time television. He flattened, and then became a point, a single orange ember, pulsing with the last of the heat and light left in him. And then nada."

#

What should have followed was a respectful

silence, but Valentin was eager to reassert himself after I had embarrassed him. "Look, Mrs. Desisada," he said, "I know it must be very hard, being the pampered wife of a diplomat. You must have all sorts of rich-people problems we normal folk could never understand. But no matter how privileged you are, you can't just make people vanish with your mind.

"Most of the time, people go crazy and the world could give tres pepinos. But you're wealthy, and your husband's important enough to be on the radar of U.N. agencies such as ours. So come with us, and we can start you on the road to recovery."

Esmeralda casts her eyes down to the table. She learned that smile from Maleficent. "If you had come alone, Xalvadora," she says, not looking up, "I would have been sure I had invented you. You are exactly the nemesis I would create for myself. Clear and professional and polite."

"Thank you," I say.

"But *him*," and her voice overflows with contempt, "him I can't account for. I have no patience for machista shit-eaters like him. All libido, no brains, all action, no forethought. Oh, no, I don't believe a word of your cover story. You might pass for a psychiatrist, Xalvadora, but there is simply no way someone as young and undisciplined as he could ever be a doctor of anything."

"I am a doctor," Valentin asserts. Esmeralda stares at him and he at her, and they contest the truth of the statement in the empty air between them.

She fills her wine from the carafe and continues. "If you are not doctors, why are you here? You might be from the U.N., some other agency, I don't know. That ID is hard to fake. Of course, if I had invented you two I would also invent a realistic ID, so by itself it proves nothing.

"It's just that *I would never invent a Valentin*. My Manuel was so gentle and thoughtful. You would have hated him, Mr. Evora. You would have had no way to understand him. I've spent my entire adult life avoiding all contact with men like you."

"You've been missing out," Valentin says with a pirate's smile.

Esmeralda sighs, then laughs, then drinks. "Shameless. I've spent this entire conversation trying to erase you from the fabric of life, and yet you persist. Why could I make a good man like Manuel vanish, but you refuse to stop existing? It's ironic, but by being unbelievable, you are forcing me to believe you."

"If Valentin is still here," I complete for her, "despite your best efforts to remove him, then there must be a world external to you. A world your mind cannot create and destroy."

"Which every sane person already knows,"

says Valentin.

Esmeralda's again glares at Valentin, shows her teeth. She turns her attention to his ID; she picks it up in her free hand and scrutinizes it. "She's a vision," Esmeralda says.

"My wife of two months."

"¿What's her name?"

"Luz. She is the light of my life."

He's forgetting his training. He's sharing too much. I reach over to grab the ID, but Esmeralda snatches it away, almost playfully. "No no no! I'm not done looking at Mr. Evora's beautiful wife. Oh, you make a lovely couple. You're both so young and strong. Without the slightest clue of the tragedies awaiting you. Now Xalvadora, she knows. Our lives are unbearable if we remember what we've done, and they are meaningless if we forget."

"Life is hard for everyone. You're speaking in platitudes."

Esmeralda shakes her head, pure mockery.

"Then welcome to your platitude," Esmeralda says, and holds up Valentin's ID to us. Luz is gone from the wedding picture. In the picture a smirking, tuxedoed Valentin is now holding air. The arm that had been behind Luz's waist in the picture is now completely visible, as if it had been Photoshopped in.

I act fast. I had invited myself over to Valentin's place five days before the mission. Valentin hadn't liked it, thought I should have gotten a hotel, but Luz was the perfect host, gracious and generous and glad to get to know her husband's partner. She was working on a degree at Miami Dade College in Aeronautical Management. She had learned to cook passably but preferred to eat out. She insisted she needed to lose 20 pounds. She had a deviated septum and would need surgery someday. She wanted a small family, two or three kids; Valentin wanted six and had their names already picked out. She said his line of work was too dangerous for six kids. What if he got himself killed? Then she would have all those mouths to feed by herself. She said all that jokingly but it was easy to see this was an old fight between them and that her fear of Valentin being killed was a private daily terror of hers.

It's enough. Luz reappears in the photo.

I don't look at him, but I can feel Valentin relax, and almost hear his tick-tock mind explaining to him it was just a momentary trick of the eye. "I'm not sure what we're supposed to be seeing, Mrs. Desisada," he says, a smirk in his voice. "Other than my ID, and my lovely wife."

Esmeralda, nonplused, looks at the ID. She puts a finger on Luz's face as says, glumly, "Okay. It's over, then. You took my power."

"We took nothing! You had no powers, vieja loca!" Valentin crows.

In a soft voice I say to her "Isn't that a good thing? You thought you had killed your husband with that power."

Sudden tears. "Oh God," she says. "Is he alive? Did I imagine it all?"

I reach across the table and open my hands. She's knows I'm about to tell her terrible news and sets down her glass and drops the wallet and puts both her hands in mine. "Your husband did die. Of a heart attack. His death precipitated your psychotic break. We've been looking for you ever since."

She weeps as openly as a child and squeezes my hands. "Please help me," she says.

"Of course." I return her squeeze and--I am not acting anymore--weep with her.

#

It's almost morning. Valentin and I are driving home to his place in his car: sporty and expensive and an unwise investment at his age. He has on allegro autotuned pop music. He thinks his first mission was a success and it's time to be happy.

We had escorted Esmeralda to the processing center. There, we sedated her and, after she was blissfully asleep, debriefed our onsite CO on the mission. He was exceedingly pleased--zero loss of life or property. "Almost unheard of with disontologicals!" he exclaimed. I told him it was too early to say that; there were a few things we needed to check first. He thought I was being modest and showered Valentin and me with promises of commendations.

We've said little to each other after leaving the processing center. But now, driving to Valentin's home, the top of the sun emerging over the horizon like a rising muffin, Valentin says to me, "That was some trick with the gun you pulled. I still don't know how you took it from me."

I have been dreading this conversation. But I cannot delay it any longer. I turn off the radio. "I didn't take your gun."

He frowns, confused. "¿Then where did my gun go?"

"Your gun is no more."

His driving suddenly improves. He'd been reckless and wreck-prone every other time I had ridden with him up to now, but as he processes my words he concentrates on the road, as if in just a few seconds he had learned to respect death. "I don't understand what you mean. A gun cannot simply disappear."

I shrug. "It did. You saw it happen yourself."

"¡Mentira!" he yells suddenly. But his outburst doesn't affect his cautious driving. It's the first time I've seen him compartmentalize his anger. "You took my gun."

"I have two guns in here," I say, opening my purse. "Try to shoot them."

"¡I'm not discharging my firearm!" he says. "They'll want to know why I'm randomly firing a gun while driving."

"Neither gun will fire for you, because they're both mine."

He glances at me twice, rapid-fire. Then, impetuously, he takes one of the guns and thrusts it out the window and at the sky and tries to shoot it. It won't fire. He drops the gun in my lap and reaches into my purse and pulls out the second Sig and he can't pull the trigger on that one either. It, too, he drops in my lap.

"Now you shoot them both," he says.

"Get in the right lane," I say, and he does. We are driving over a bridge; the ocean is to our right. I lower the automatic window and take a gun in each hand and fire both of them in unison. Then I put the safety on the guns and put them back in the purse and raise the window. We are over the bridge and almost to his townhouse.

"This could still be a trick," he says. "You could have brought two guns."

"I suppose that is true" I answer slowly. "It's

not what happened, but it could have, and I don't have a good way to prove to you it didn't, amy more than what I have shown you. But if you choose to believe me now, we may save your wife."

"What?!" We pull off the road and into a parking space in front of his townhouse. He shuts off the car and turns to me, his tie askew and the buttons on his shirt strained to bursting.

"I don't know what Esmeralda attacked," I say evenly. "Maybe just the photo. But maybe Luz."

Realization. Terror. Valentin desperately reaches into his coat and pulls out his wallet. Relief. "She's still here!"

"Re-realizing photos is easy," I say. "They're simple for me. Compared to a real live person."

Valentin launches himself out of the car toward his townhouse door. I throw myself out, too, and block his path to his apartment and grab his arms.

"No!" I yell. "Not with fear. With faith. Look at me. Your wife is there behind that door. She is going to serve us mediocre but made-with-love eggs, and as we eat she'll tell us how her classes have been going, and you're going to nag her about wanting a big family, and she's going to complain she's overweight, and life will continue just as you thought it would. Believe, Valentin. Believe or she's already lost."

"Okay," he says. "Of course. ¡Coño! Of course!" He takes out his keys and looks at me once more, and I do my best to return to him the surety he lent me earlier, his unshakable belief in the truth of world that accidentally saved my life and his. He marches toward the door and unlocks it and stands in its jamb and calls out, "I'm home, Luz! ¿Are you awake? ¿Where are you, mi vida?" He's so desperate to know he runs into the house without turning on the lights.

Esmeralda had to be taken into custody I

think. *Esmeralda had to be taken into custody.*

I stand outside surrounded the dying-fire glow of the coming morning. But the sunlight just hides the doorway in deeper shadows.

END

Pitching Shemp
by James Beamon

The Widower Burney stood over the casket shuddering with sobs and bawling his eyes out, behavior which could only ruin my photo. I expected a quiet sniffle, a quick dab of his eyes before he sat back down to enjoy his recent widowerhood with some damn dignity. No, the dude seemed to be one "auugh" away from jumping into the casket with his late wife. I looked around the room of my funeral home and it was apparent that none of these people were friends enough to rein this guy in. Well if they didn't care, neither did I, but... I needed the pic.

I pulled up beside Mr. Burney. He was doing that stuttering sniffle-gasp thing that crying toddlers do after their parents tell them to shut up but they physically can't. "She's... suh... suh... so... suh... suh... beaut... suh... suh... suh... tiful!"

I nodded. As a black man born and raised in Mississippi, I knew not to take credit for a white woman's beauty, even if things were much more progressive now than when I was a kid, and even if I had poured hours into making the late Mrs. Burney look as fine as baby hair. I had seen something special in her bone structure and made it a point to style her to look like a young Rita Hayworth. Her red hair had that thick curl action going, like it was a bed you could just lay in. Maybe that's what was making Mr. Burney act like he was fixing to try.

The problem with not taking credit for making her more attractive than his recent memory could recall was the obvious lack of credit. People don't think about all the work that goes into post-mortem beautification and eventually they assume the shit happened naturally, like she magically went from blue to buttercup blossoms simply 'cause I got her into her favorite dress. I may not say thanks, but I still remind them who the magician is.

"If you've enjoyed her presentation, please tell your friends about me."

"Huh?" he asked, bewildered.

My eyes panned around the ceiling. "Gotta keep the lights on. Word of mouth business and all."

He nodded. I took that as acquiescence to promote my business so I took out my phone and snapped a pic of my little Rita lookalike. Out of the corner of my eye, I could see the bereaved husband and I could almost see his wheels turning, wondering what the hell I was doing.

"Portfolios don't build themselves," I said gravely, as if I was saying "sorry for your loss."

Pic secured, I left him to bawl. As a mortician, it was my professional duty to let him wail to his heart's content or until his two-hour viewing window was up. As a veteran of marriage, however, I wanted to tell him to cheer up, that the war was over, and that he had won. They put that "er" on the end of "widower" because she must've made a mistake if the man outlived her. There's no special gender designation for divorcees, just saying.

Once I had returned to the corner of the parlor, I dug out my phone and sent the pic to Bob Karloff. A shadow loomed over me, and I knew Mojo's titan-sized ass had come over.

"Way to play up the creepy mortician, Pops, taking pictures in front of everybody," he whispered. "Now they all probably thinking you're a necrophiliac. I'm surprised you didn't feel her up while you were at it, you know, really drive it home."

"Please," I whispered back. "If I wanted cold and lifeless, I would've stayed with your mother."

"Leave mom out of this. She ain't the one looking like a right pervert."

I shrugged at my son. "You know I had to get the pic. Last thing either one of us wants is another Shemp."

A moment later, my cell phone buzzed. Bob Karloff's reply:

A RITA HAYWORTH! DEFINITELY A MUST PROCURE.

I showed Mojo. He grinned. Another step closer to heaven.

Soon as the viewing was over and it was time for the funeral service, we went to work. I politely drew the curtains separating the stage where the coffin sat from the mourning onlookers. The coffin sat on a long cabinet stand and now, safe from prying eyes, I opened the cabinet doors on the stand to reveal twenty odd gallon jugs filled with dirt. Mojo pulled Mrs. Burney from her beautiful mahogany wood coffin and dragged her over to the supply closet. I replaced the body with fifteen dirt jugs and closed the coffin lid while Mojo stuffed fistfuls of Hollywood starlet-grade cadaver into the closet and latched it shut.

We opened the curtains together, smooth as if we were on the honor guard, our well-honed process to swap a body taking all of two minutes. Handling the gallon jugs made for a much smoother process than our older method of loading giant dirt bags. Besides, it was nice to repurpose those empty milk cartons, go green and shit. Only drawback was me and Mojo were going to have to up our intake of Honey Nut Cheerios if we wanted to be ready for the next corpse grab.

I gave a curt nod toward the pall bearers and stepped out of the way. Six men stepped upon the stage with white gloves. Theirs was the noble task of bearing a casket of dirt jugs out of the funeral home and en route to its final resting place.

My tasks were less noble and involved selling a body and buying more milk. It started with Bob Karloff, who would likely arrive in less than twenty minutes with the way he travels. Once all the funeral goers had filed out in the wake of the casket, Mojo and I went over to the tiny broom closet. Mrs. Burney was slumped down, her face thrust in a mop.

Mojo took her arms, I grabbed some ankles and we took her downstairs to the workshop in the basement. The space was unusually cluttered with boxes of embalming and taxidermy supplies stacked on the workbench and around the floor.

I wanted to put her in a chair but Mojo scoffed at the idea. "With her head flopping around on her neck like a watermelon glued to a slinky? Nah. Ain't no way to treat a starlet. I got something special. Let her go."

I released her ankles and Mojo carried her over to the corner where Shemp stood. If I recalled correctly, Shemp had been a farmer in life but now he was long dead, stuffed and made to look exactly like the third stooge thanks to Bob Karloff's advanced alien tech. The tech had also made Shemp poseable, like a giant action figure. Right now Shemp had his arms bent at ninety degrees, both hands giving us pointed finger guns. Mojo stood Rita up between Shemp's arms and I couldn't see much else as my son's bulky frame took up the whole of the corner.

When he finally came away, he kept a self-satisfied smirk on his face as Shemp held Rita. One of Shemp's hands lovingly cradled the back of her neck and head. The other hand firmly gripped her ass. Her eyes were closed as if she was waiting for that magical first kiss. Shemp ignored her and stared ahead at us, a sloppy grin on his face as if he had just won the lottery.

"Man, I wanna post this on my Facebook," Mojo said.

I looked at his display, the evidence of which would get us hemmed up with multiple counts of grave robbing, defiling a corpse, and who the hell knew what else.

"Yeah, me too," I said.

"Greetings," a harsh voice called from upstairs. "It is Bob, coming down your stairs to you." A clomp, clomp, clomp followed until Bob Karloff stood at the base of the stairs. He wore a trenchcoat.

He went by Bob, just Bob, because it was a pretty common name. Everybody knows a Bob, right? But we called him Bob Karloff because we already knew like three Bobs before we had made his acquaintance and because he was a scary looking motherfucker. Fake blue eye contacts stuck over large red eyes, a brown toupee that sat high on his head and resembled a run over squirrel, lips like chapped little razors, skin like melted cheese. He looked like either an alien in human guise or the target demographic for phone sex lines.

"Moses Monroe," he greeted me with a stiff nod. I returned the gesture, albeit more smoothly. He turned to my son. "Moses Monroe Junior," he greeted my son. "Where is the Rita Hayworth?"

As if we had practiced for it, me and Mojo held our hands out at the same time toward Shemp and Rita. Bob didn't smile, but his eyes got bigger and a bit redder behind the contacts, which was the Paedian equivalent. He went over and gave Rita a four-point inspection.

"Yes, she does nicely fit. I procure immediately."

He produced a small jar from inside his trench coat. He opened the jar and placed it under Rita's nose. The nanomachines look like a shimmery silver mist as they left the jar and flew up her nose. Within moments Mrs. Burney's face began to change slightly, with the cheeks becoming more pronounced, the nose more aquiline, her lips more pouty, redder until she had become as much Rita Hayworth as the original had been in her heyday. New Rita opened her eyes.

"Extricate yourself from Shemp," Bob Karloff instructed. "Go to wait by the stairs."

Rita silently headed out, returning Shemp to his abject state of bachelorhood. "So what's the balance?" I asked Bob.

He produced a tablet from his trenchcoat much shinier than Apple's shiniest tablet. "Rita Hayworth sells for 2500 GSU, immediately credited to your account. By my calculations, you only need a thousand more to afford onboarding."

One thousand Galactic Standard Units was nothing. I mean it was really nothing on Earth, where we were still tossing paper around like kids trading bottlecaps. But even among the advanced spacefaring civilizations, a thousand GSU was easy enough to get. Someone really niche like Angela Lansbury in her "Murder She Wrote" phase or the husband on "Bewitched" sold for over a thousand. This meant only one more corpse stood between us and two tickets to emigrate.

"That's great news," I said. I smiled and pointed a thumb to the back corner. "You sure you can't use a Shemp?"

The alien didn't even look at him. "Fuck Shemp."

I sighed. Goddamn Shemp. Maybe I was bitter from the complete lack of buyers, but I felt that Shemp brought his own unique comedy styling to the act. How was I supposed to know a whole galaxy of sentient beings preferred Curly? Shemp stayed in the corner, a constant reminder to always take a picture and make the sell before we go through the trouble of snatching a corpse out of the casket.

Bob Karloff must have seen the disappointment on my face. "Cheer yourself," he said. "People on Earth, they die all the time. One of them will eventually be of resemblance to a filmed persona. Earth has so many actors, so many actresses, so many stories! It is after all your chief export. So increase your cheer, the end is in fist."

He made a fist and showed it to me like he was part of the black power movement. Bless his heart; learning idiomatic English was not on a Paedian's list of priorities. He was right about a couple things, though. We die all the time. And the one thing we did better than virtually the whole galaxy was tell stories.

I figured maybe it was some kind of evolutionary thing, like the left brain develops more and more as civilizations advance. The science and logic centers of the left brain probably go much further in building faster-than-light spaceships than the poetry and finger painting centers of the right brain. Don't get me wrong, sometimes both hemispheres team up to do powerful shit, like when a legion of concerned male scientists came together to knock out erectile dysfunction with blue and purple pills. We beat that before we beat cancer, and you can't tell me the passion and love areas over in right brain didn't have a hand in that, just saying.

Bob Karloff put down his black power fist and left with his new Rita Hayworth. He'd get her back to Paed, to his shop where a diverse, interstellar public would be able to buy her to put her in home brewed, horribly scripted movies. This was how aliens did fanfic, because writing it was just too barbaric for the technologically minded.

After Bob Karloff left, me and Mojo high fived each other and hugged it out with Shemp.

Everything felt like gravy until tomorrow afternoon, when a dude that looked like a hard drinker in a cheap suit showed up. His five o'clock shadow had definitely made it to eight o'clock and his red tie hung loose around his collar, like he couldn't be bothered to tighten.

"Who's running this place?" he asked me.

I figured maybe someone died given his grizzled appearance, so I quietly hoped for back to back famous faces when I introduced myself. Then he brought out his badge and I felt a bag of butterflies weighted with rocks sinking in the pit of my stomach.

"Detective John Bowser," he said putting the badge away. "I need your guys to dig up a stiff you just put in the ground yesterday. One Amanda Burney." After he said that he fished into his blazer pocket for what was undoubtedly the court order.

"Holy hell!" I swore before straightening my composure into one that was more somber and mortician-ish. "This is unpleasant news, disturbing the final rest and all." I shook my head gravely as I took the court order.

"Meh. She'll live. Well, I guess not, but she's gonna have to get over it anyway."

The court order was unfortunately both legit and airtight. I couldn't find a reason to say no. I needed a reason bad. "May I ask why she needs to be exhumed?"

"You can ask, but don't expect any answers, undertaker. Closed investigation."

"I need to know what my staff is dealing with, in case you're asking them to handle dangerous biological or chemical agents. It's one thing to handle a buried casket, another thing entirely to ask my staff to expose themselves to Agent Orange or Ebola-pox."

Detective Bowser grimaced. He seemed to chew on the point I made like it was gristle. Finally, he nodded. "Nothing to worry about, suspicion of poison. Totally non-contagious. Satisfied?"

I forced a smile. "I'm afraid it's going to take a couple days. We have to coordinate our diggers, schedule the exhumation. I'm sure you understand."

"Hell if I do. You're authorized twenty-four hours to prep, then I want this shit popping like bacon grease, you follow?" He pointed over to my son who was filling up the doorframe behind me. "Get the Green Mile over there to help you. I bet a shovel looks like a spoon in his hands."

Detective Bowser snatched the court order from me and stalked off, probably to find a bar. Mojo came over, his jaw tight.

"This is bad."

I had nothing to say in response. I tried to think of a way around it but I couldn't get the first thought on how to do that started. My mind was empty like all the infinite deep I'd never get to travel to.

"It's not too late, Pops," Mojo said. "We can still cash those GSUs in for diamonds and gold, head to the Caribbean and enjoy Earth style filthy richness."

"No, it is too late," I countered. "It takes time to move diamonds and gold. 'Suddenly found' treasures have a way of making headlines. The last thing we need to make are headlines when tomorrow this cop is going to open a casket full of dirt jugs. We need a plan."

Beyond the impossible time crunch, resigning ourselves to Earthly living seemed so drab in comparison. Bob Karloff had taken us on a trip to Paed and a few other galactic hotspots a couple years back. After that trip, I felt I had been living my whole life as a kid in some backwater village, one of those places you didn't know existed until you see a commercial for the Peace

Corps. Bob Karloff was like one of the volunteers from the Peace Corps who took me back to America and showed me a supermarket, cars, the Internet. It was hard to go back to the village.

Maybe Bob could get us out of this. I looked at my phone and grimaced. Space travel involved quantum states, which meant Bob was both here and not here until you tried to observe him. My cell phone company's billing algorithms were the ones observing Bob, so I either got hit with a local call or the most extreme long distance had to offer, the kind of billing that's usually talked about after an asterisk before you sign the contract.

I bit the bullet and dialed. Bob answered immediately.

"You procure another already?"

"No. Listen, we need to emigrate now."

"You do not have the necessary GSUs to afford on-boarding."

"It's only a thousand. Be a pal. Let me hold something."

"This holding sounds like an idiom for borrowing units. If so, no."

"C'mon! Don't be a dick, Bob. I'll pay you back."

"I will always be a Bob, never a dick. This Bob will not be paid back because he will not loan units. Is that all you called for?"

"I called because I need your help, Bob. Tomorrow a police officer is going to dig up the grave of your new Rita Hayworth, discover the missing body and put me and Mojo under the jail. We're not only going to be stuck on Earth, but in the worst place on Earth. You know that's no way to be with a business partner. Help us out."

After tense moments of silence, Bob's voice crackled over the phone. "I think I have an idea, one which will help you and the Fantasy Fanfic

Guild that meets in my shop twice a week. See you in six hours or so."

#

Bob Karloff's plan, stitched together by his desire to turn a profit, was audacious. He was going to scare the cop away along with any associated diggers by charging the Fantasy Fanfic Guild a fee to film a horror movie on location in a sanctioned Earth graveyard. Not even cops were trained to handle a dozen or more deceased Hollywood stars back from the dead in a graveyard. It was a scene anyone would run from. Maybe the cop would never come back. I mean, how do you report seeing Lon Chaney, Audrey Hepburn, Marlon Brando and James Dean descend upon you in a graveyard?

"This is amazingly creative, considering," Mojo said.

"Sure," I agreed. What I didn't speak on was that I recognized the plan as the starting premise of every episode of Scooby Doo, where something seemingly supernatural scares off the townies. But as long as it worked he could've lifted it from "A Charlie Brown Christmas" for all I cared.

We toured the night time graveyard with Bob Karloff. Unlike most advanced aliens, Bob had spent a few years developing a tolerance for Earths' unique blend of domestic bacteria in a nitrogen rich atmosphere so he coordinated the shoot on the ground while the aliens who comprised the Fantasy Fanfic Guild stayed safely aloft in spacecraft hidden by overcast skies. Right now he was panning his shiny tablet around, feeding the guild imagery.

"How much you charging them for your services?" I asked Bob as he ran his tablet slowly by some headstones.

"Six thousand GSUs per guild member per hour," he answered.

"Can I get a cut?"

"No. That is like paying you to do you a favor."

I was about to see if I could squeeze a few units out of the cheapskate, when a flashlight beam in the distance stole my attention. A silhouette of a person with a shovel came into view. The person was heading our way.

"Hide," I whispered.

We fell back a ways and hid behind some angel statues. A couple minutes plodded by with the silhouette growing ever closer until the person stopped at the grave of Mrs. Burney. At this distance, he was no longer a silhouette but the widower Mr. Burney.

"I knew it!" I whispered. "All those waterworks was a show. He poisoned his wife and now he's going to try to dig her up before the cops can get to her."

I turned to Bob Karloff who was hunkered down beside me and looking at his tablet. "Can you get some footage of him digging up the grave?" I asked. I figured if I timed it right, I could get some evidence of Mr. Burney digging up the grave, then chase him off, then call the cops and say the husband took the body. I don't know if the new plan was exactly airtight, but it seemed to let less air out than Scooby Doo.

"Yes, we will have footage aplenty," Bob Karloff whispered taking his eyes off the tablet. "The guild is going now, they say."

I was going to ask what the hell that meant when a woman's voice cut through the quiet behind Burney.

"After all this time, we finally meet, Mister, to a tune you won't get away with."

Burney spun around. The woman behind him was bathed in darkness. Before Burney could bring his flashlight to bear upon her, a giant beam of light blasted down from the overcast sky to reveal his recently dead wife, who looked more like Rita Hayworth now than Mrs.

Burney, especially in that red cocktail dress she wore.

Burney looked at his dead wife, then up to the sky where the light beam terminated into dark clouds, then back at his wife. He dropped the shovel.

The guild wasn't done, not yet. Another massive beam of light erupted from the sky, revealing Humphrey Bogart. He wore his signature trench coat.

"You should've seen the expression plastered all over your coffee mug, Bub," Bogie said. "The press is gonna have a field day with this one."

Before Mr. Burney could adjust to seeing Casablanca era Humphrey Bogart, another beam of light blasted from the clouds. The beam highlighted the Cowardly Lion. The lion suit was flawless.

"You don't have to do this, nyah nyah. Just let the girl go. We can settle this once and for all. Put 'em up, put 'em up!"

Another beam burst out of the sky. Michael Jackson was on the ground end of it, Thriller style in the red jacket with a hundred zippers. "Beat it," he said to all the previous stars that came before. "Can't you see he's bad? He's dangerous." He emphasized the danger with a kick followed by a pelvic thrust.

Another beam came down to highlight Danny Glover as he appeared in every Danny Glover movie. "I'm getting too old for this shit," he said.

Mojo nudged me. "Danny Glover ain't even dead yet. Dammit, Pops, we could've been off this planet years ago if they would've told us we could use living people. Remember that dude we buried that looked like Kevin Bacon? And that chick a month ago that looked like Taylor Swift? What the hell?"

Meanwhile more and more stars kept coming, heralded by a beam of light from on high. The upper atmosphere was starting to resemble

Swiss cheese as celebrities both living and dead appeared to deliver clichéd dialogue.

This had gotten out of hand a dozen stars ago. Now Michael Jackson had a dance troupe facing off against Fred Astaire like some bizarre West Side Story. In the middle of the dance floor cemetery battleground, the widower Burney huddled against his wife's gravestone, eyes wide. He was shivering like a dog shitting razor blades.

"Oh my god!" Mojo cried, pointing at one of the white dudes in the dance off. He looked at Bob Karloff with accusation in his eyes. "There's a market for the guy that does Riverdance but nobody wants to buy Shemp?!"

"Michael Flatley is a genius," Bob Karloff stated.

Apparently these two had no problem with the ongoing chaos, but I had had enough. I stood up to stop the madness. "Hold it!" I screamed. "Quiet! Cut! Stop!" I yelled, waving my arms as

I made my way toward Burney. He looked beyond cracked.

I went to help him up. I didn't think that crazy may also mean hostile. Too late I saw the gun. It went off like thunder.

"Get away from me!" Burney cried. Pain stabbed my gut. My legs felt like jello. I collapsed to the ground.

An instant later all the celebrities surrounded by light were sucked up into the sky. I guess the Fantasy Fanfic Guild members didn't want to risk property damage with a nutjob blasting holes into people. Burney took this sudden absence of star power as a cue to leave and he booked.

Mojo rushed over. He took off his jacket and held it against my wound to stop the tide of blood.

"Stop, Mojo," I said. I had dealt with death too many times to not recognize what was coming soon. Thankfully, I was growing numb to the pain. "Looks like we solved the problem," I said with a wan smile. I looked at Bob Karloff. "One ticket to on-board, already paid for with units to spare, yes?"

Bob Karloff nodded. "Indeed."

I faced my son again. "See to it that I get the fanfic treatment. I'd rather kick it around the galaxy as a life-sized action figure than be in a box down here. OK?"

"Sure, Pops," Mojo said behind wet eyes.

"I want you to make a movie. Tell our story."

Mojo nodded solemnly. Maybe this was meant to be. If the rest of the galaxy made movies as bad as the Fantasy Fanfic Guild, Mojo would undoubtedly become a filmmaking legend throughout the universe.

"Just promise me one thing," I said.

"Anything, Pops."

I thought of the one man who could've gotten us out of this whole mess. Thoughts of his revenge made me smile.

"Make sure Shemp is in it."

END

Sand's Speaking Solemn
by Sierra July

Glasga has vials set along the shelves of her crack-walled settle room, fed thirty sand grains a piece, exact. Temporary placement, be sure. She'd have to pick them up again to prepare for the move, cork their mouths and shove them in the dark of her sack-it. 'Fore that she let 'em breathe.

Land Lady's come in to clean and is dusting away at the vials like she plans to sweep away their insides.

"What do you do with this dirt? Most go out, gather hides. Meat to eat, fur to barter, that's living. You, you stock on fecal matter."

"'Tis clean. I dig two meters 'fore I collect. Get it wet and cold, let it dry by sun."

"But for what? You store dirt to gather dust?"

Ignoring is easy. Glasga is pro at the art. Had to be to get over the ha-has she got from other young Journeyers, snickers, giggles bombarding her. Glasga had collected sand since she was a little munchkin (that's what her maman called her), little gal at age five and a day. It was just after her fifth birthday that she was allowed to travel the lands bordering her home place. Yes, she was meant to learn to kill, pack pounds on her light bones and hides in her sack-it, but she had reason for her lack of doing. None could understand, not her fellow Journeyers, not this Land Lady, nor the next in lands a year's length over. Papan, now he got it.

"I'll come back tomorrow night."

"I'll be gone then."

"Ah, well! This will be the last I see of your dirt then. Good riddance."

The woman slams the door on her way out. Glasga hopes the other habitants come complaining to the *kuh* about the noise. She undresses (dismantles the body armor nestling under her shawls, sheds her headscarf and medallions) and climbs into bed. Her sands lull her to sleep. The crisp azure of Ladle's Bend, the hypnotic burgundy of Xilos, the greys of Parapluie Plain where the sky matched the land and cast all in monochrome. She'd have time to hold them to morning's light if she woke early, see 'em beam.

Curled into a ball of sheets, she finds her dreams.

#

"I thank you for my stay." Glasga bows.

"I thank *you* to be gone."

Glasga almost turns away angry, but spots tears creeping in the Land Lady's eyes. How long had it been since the old *kuh* had a worthy opponent? Too long, long as Glasga's been seeking out her sands.

"I mean my words, Land Lady. I thank you."

"Yes, yes, now be gone with you. And don't return lest you clean yourself of that dirt."

Sad . . . to Glasga that invitation meant never.

Sun high comes too soon. Used as her feet are to travel, the ground burns them. This terrain's stoned face doesn't help none. It mocks her 'cause it leaves her with no grains to sample. Seems it's shining, bouncing light back into her eyes and they're starting to paint freckles on the landscape. She saps water from the gourd that occupies her sack-it and keeps going. Dots, dots, dots eating away her vision . . .

'Fore she can watch herself, her foot catches a crack in the ground and she tumbles. She hisses and gets right back on her feet. That crack was too wide to be sun damage. It doesn't take much study to tell her it's the work of a Desegator. Rumors say one wrong move and it'll pop up and snare a limb, and that wasn't even the kicker. Its teeth seeped venom powerful 'nough to see a three-ton dragon keel in ten minutes, gal her size would be done in quarter-minute. She'd have only an instant to try an' dodge.

Despite the threat looming under her, she looks at the sky. Cloud cover, that's what she needed, a moment's shade . . . Yes!

She darts back from the crack and doubles over in relief. Desegators required light to catch their prey. Night tranquilized them, as did shade. She turns to carry on and sees more wide chasms about her, a maze of Desegator-dug landmines. Getting away from this many, with the sun now uncovered and no new patch for its cyclop's eye in sight, would take a Razorwing's snatching her up and lifting her off with its blink-and-miss speed; since they were extinct, that was pure hoping.

Stock-still she stays 'til she thinks her bones will steel, 'til her blood feels to have hardened with them and her legs have grown stiff, 'til she can't stay steady any longer, and her foot shifts.

There, there is her leg being shredded off, poison causing her every nerve ending to shiver in heated pain, the agony of her teeth being plucked, her hair being yanked, cuts, burns, eyes skewered.

But none of that came.

'Fore her stood a Desegator, yes, a bottle-necked rocket on four scaled feet. Yet it didn't budge, just stared. If she moved this time, Glasga knew she'd lose, fight, journey, life over. She takes a slow breath and waits.

She's going good an hour's past (still no cloud cover), hasn't wriggled a toe. But her mind reels; that she can't keep from moving. She scans the creature, analyzes its every claw.

Never has she set eye on the creature 'fore now of course, (it would have meant she was clinging to the earth in spirit) but fables told again and again have given her expert knowledge. This specimen is a foot's length long when Desegator's were said to span five. It has but four legs when it ought to carry six. Eyes . . . its eyes are twin in shade to the soft blue of Ladle's Bend, not ember red. It is an anomaly.

She has no confidence in the idea but she figures a peculiar creature calls for peculiar action. She sways, breezing to the left. When nothing happens, she steps, steps again.

Then the creature springs.

It lands atop her bare foot and cocks its head, beautiful and ugly.

"Are you a young one, Desegator?"

Chirrrup.

Its reply, a siren shriek of a chirp, shakes her nerves but she keeps chatting.

"As I thought, either you have yet to obtain your venom or you know not how to use it. Put her here."

She extends her hand and the Desegator shimmies up to her shoulder. Any sane woman or mann would feel threatened. Looking at its glassy orbs for eyes, Glasga can't bring herself to. Death had its fists around her every day and all it had to do was clutch tighter. She'd lost fear on the doorstep of maman's settle-down, only place she knew felt permanent, lost it to the stone cuts brought on by rock-pelting youngsters that had already determined she was odd by day one, lost in tears and blood. If she was going, she was going by the hands (claws) of her first buddy-friend.

"Bet you carved all these trenches yourself. Guess digging runs in both our veins. You come with me and we'll roam a bit a ways more 'fore nightfall."

Her creature nods (or it appears that way) and they carry on.

#

Stars and moons blanket the sky and Glasga stretches back to marvel their dance, Desegator nuzzled in the crook of her arm.

"You have thirty gold scales about your eyes, my fated number. My maman gave birth to me at thirty years and my papan died at thirty years. Thirty grains, that's how much sand I collect, just 'nough so a hair's width of the vial bottom is covered. You wanna know why?"

"*Chirpp.*"

"You's about the first creature, human or beast, to care. My papan was a humungous mann, shook the ground he walked on, humungous 'nough you could scarce hold the love of him in your heart. All loved him, he grinned happy so. He built humans of wood, stood them up around our settle-down, and anyone else's who wanted 'em. Such living wooden people! I remember gawking at 'em, hearing 'em talk. But just a month short of my journey date, my fifth birthday, he turned to dust. Maman had him buried so that he could end that way.

I looked at sand different thereafter, asked about, read up on it. Desperate, I crept upon a book cracked and abandoned in the crevice of a deceased neighbor's settle-down. Who knows how long it sat. 'Haps the old woman forgot it was even in her possession. It was the sort of text that should have wound up charred. In it I read on a sand magic. 'One that can restore things lost,' it said. Don't know exactly what it means, but my papan's lost. Might be those grains of sand magic can bring him back. I tell anyone this and they say I got dirt mudding up my brain, say that book was of the made-up kind. But if there's a chance, a chance dwarfed by a grain of sand, I'm gonna take it."

Glasga gazes down at the Desegator, discovers he's asleep.

"You're forgiven, little friend. Might be you saved me a blush, not listening. Ridiculous, 'haps, but it's my story and I've got to see it end."

Glasga rests down her head and is about to shut her eyes when she senses it, a rumbling carrying on the land that rattles her bones. "Little friend," she whispers. "Trouble."

To her surprise the Desegator's eyes pop open, all aglow and so intense his pupils are contracting in the dim light. Her eyes 'haps are doing it too because all at once she can see them coming, the Pferde.

In a heartbeat, here they are, surrounding her on all four corners.

The bronze-colored monsters hiss as they shake sand grains from their long head-hairs and stamp their half-moon feet as though impatient to get back to storming with their lightning speed. But it's their riders that have Glasga biting her lip.

They have no mouths to speak and no eyes worth seeing, so neither she nor no one living knows what they're thinking or what they want, but everyone in this land knows they come. Everything's empty where a face should be, empty like a pit; Glasga can't have imagined it from the yarns she'd heard before, but here it is, as described, the face of nothing. Human, animal, or spirit, there's just no say what the riders are.

She sets a glance on her Desgator to see how he feels about all these happenings-on and sees he's back on the sand, asleep, passed out, or dead from shock. She feels she could keel too but focuses on not showing it. Might be no one could get away from the Pferde without bleeding to death a day later, but no one else was her. She focuses on slipping her right hand to her waist, grabbing the shaft of the knife she keeps tucked in folds of her outer garments. Her only weapon and her only prayer, the knife is too puny to shake great enemies, even now she isn't sure it'll be enough.

The first of the Pferde descends his monster and all the others cop-cat him, leaving their beasts' hides. Then they're coming, slow as shadows 'cross the ground, their feet so hushed Glasga misses their sound. They're pressing up on her, closer, closer still . . .

A pain sears through her leg and she realizes her chance to strike has come and gone. She crumbles into mush only half aware that there are unnatural sounds dancing 'bout, sounds between piggy cries and kiddy squeals and maniac laughs. It's all a jumble, but when she opens her eyes again all she's got for company are empty clothes 'ready being snatched by the wind, and her Desegator's grin. Haps her mind is teasing but she's sure she sees that little devil wink.

She shakes the muddle from her head, shakily gets back to standing. She glances down at her leg wound and recognizes it's still spewing her life out aplenty. It's too quick and mighty to stop and she's too worn to try. Her gut and mind tell her to resist, keep trying.

She can't.

Glasga collapses on the sand, her hand still trying to clutch her leg wound as her vision fades.

#

Glasga wakes to heat, but not just from the sun. She looks about and sees Desegator, huffing hot air for all he's worth on her wound . . . to what was her wound. Where a gorge was made in her skin now sits a shallow scratch.

She sits up, flexes her leg and finds the sore and tired has been whisked out of it. She can stand and walk, run if she has to.

"I owe you heaps now, buddy-friend. Much as I owe maman and papan for life. Stick close and I'll see 'bout paying it back."

The Desegator looks to nod then scrambles up her, hiding from the sun she notes is now centered high in the sky. She smiles a mite and off they go.

#

The next town winks at them beyond hillside, earth shifting from dirty brown steel to a jade carpet, plush 'nough to melt beneath Glasga's toes. If it is a breed of sand, never has she felt one so waxy, seen grain particles so large and wide and proud they stretch their hands to heaven. The Desegator braces itself against her neck as she stoops to inspect. Plucking a handful of green grain shows her that true soil lies underneath, same shade as the lands past but clumped with moisture. Curiosity gnaws her so she could set there and shred the green carpet till moon high, but a likeness of her papan burns behind her eyes. From then on, she has no trouble carrying on.

The green ends on a line of crimson sand, border of town. People bustle on the other side, chattering, guffawing. None have yet taken her notice.

"Come, little friend, can't have none casting sight on you."

Glasga stuffs the Desegator in her shrouds, against her bosom. She feels one clawed foot against her skin, piercing just over her heart, and is obliged to her body armor. If a bite was death, a puncture from its daggered toes was goodbye to her soul. Word of mouth says if a Desegator gets to the home of your soul, you won't wake in this world or in any next; you evaporate in air.

"I'm trusting you, hear?"

"Chirrup."

"Then let's go."

Head high, Glasga strides like she has nothing to hide. Settle rooms lean tired on weary wooden legs, roofs of straw bearing patches. Settle-downs appear more permanent (as they should) enforced with stone blocks along their foundations. Children cling to their maman's skirts 'though there isn't much there to cling to. Women here are less adorned than she's used to, unhindered by sun and wind. Their arms are tanned as hers from sun baking, 'though slack and tame, beautiful but untrained. In contrast, men are bulging boulders, muscles rippling. All wear grins too broad for their faces. She frowns and trudges on.

She spots a decent settle room, one which should bear her weight for the evening, and speaks to the Land Lady.

"May I rest in your care?"

"Just you?"

"That's right, ma'am. I'm a Journeyer."

"You? Then where are your hides."

"I sold them all a town over. I'll be hunting for more come a new day."

"Very well. In my care, you nest."

Glasga takes to her room, but can't swallow her guilt at stretching truth for the Land Lady.

She'd tackled stocking hides but it wasn't for her. She can recall her first kill. Invigorated by the stalk and chase, the takedown was same as breathing, effortless. Meat from a Boundeer danced sweet on her tongue, quenching as pure water. But night came and she couldn't get the stench of blood and guts from her hands and hair. She witnessed the light drain from the creature's eyes, same that had been prancing, tail high, ears pricked, 'fore she'd encountered it. One, two kills later, she cast aside the art. Food came to her from others hands, dried for storage, browned for immediate munchies.

Her room is bland as anyplace, white walls and sheets, bare floors. She empties her sack-it of her vials, establishes them one-by-one to her windowsill. It is a tight squeeze but they're used to hugging. Her heart skips studying them. They are all that anoint this place with a settle-down feel. Well, all but for a sweet scent perfume in the air.

Glasga notices a tall glass with little faces peeping out, yellow dots with manes of lilac circling them like bonnets. They stand on green stick bodies with hands that poke out like the carpet from the soil outside town. Whatever they were, their aroma was good as eating, causing her stomach hunger pains.

Her Desegator hops from her dressings and chows on a fancy face, chomping happy.

"Taste good, Desegator? These can't be your normal diet, not where you're from. I've never seen such things."

She takes one up herself, bites down on it. An acid bitterness assaults her tongue and she spits her fancy face out, willing to spit some more in the tall glass to dispel the flavors lingering.

"You can eat these all by yourself. I'm getting true food."

She moves to the door and the Desegator moves with her.

"You're better off setting yourself here. Can't guarantee you won't be gutted out there."

"Chirrup. Chi-Chir."

It scurries up her leg, ducks under her clothing back into its hiding spot.

"All right but you better steady yourself. I have some sand collecting to do."

#

Stomach satisfied with wild Hoxen on rye (bartered for with dried Salamadile tails she'd held on to for weeks), Glasga explores the green carpet before collecting sand. 'Haps it won't look bad in her collection, just a few plucks . . .

"You're never seen grass before?"

A mann towers behind her with his hands on his hips, gawking with a smirk.

"I've journeyed far but not so that I've seen all that lies upon it."

"Yes. But there are books for you, for anyone, to educate themselves with."

"Reading is a start, a big leap in learning, but knowledge comes from smelling, tasting, feeling. You can't know the power of a loaf till you're had one feed your mouth, fill your stomach."

"'Haps so. You know it's rare to see a female Journeyer? That's what you are right, a new and short-lived passerby?"

"In my home place, male and female are lead to journey. Finding one's self depends on crossing borders, seeing sights, meeting people, all in childhood. We return when ready 'though some never return, lost, dead, or taken new residence is wisdom unknown."

"Intriguing . . . Is that a Desegator?"

Her Desegator has broken from hiding and is springing across what the mann called 'grass.' It circles back, passing Glasga and heading towards town. She sees what it is after: a scarlet Snakeel bathing itself in red sand, masking itself from nearby food vendors so that it can get easy meals of its own, snapping up food dropped, forgotten and forsaken. The Desegator is taking strides to reach its prey while Glasga holds her breath, praying no one (besides the mann alongside her) sees it.

She needn't have worried for the town's eyes are on the skies, and the shadow of a creature blotching it out.

"It's a Vulawk!

"A Vulawk!"

"Get children, inside. Everyone, inside!"

Roars, hectic shrieks vibrate through the town and Glasga's Desegator still runs. The mann who'd stood beside her has already moved to take shelter. She takes one look up at the underside of great black wings and sprints for her little friend.

"What are doing? Get out of there!"

She hears the mann's warning even through the chaos, somehow thundering though all else muted. No one had handed her warnings before,

no one had cared. (*Kuh! Kuh*, got a screw loose!)
Jeers, sneers from teeth glistening with bitter
spit, sharp tongues, hateful. Had any came at
her with warnings, they were to turn back, run
away, forfeit. Yes, the mann's were the same.
She hadn't heeded them then and wouldn't now.

Rather than diving for her friend, she aims
for a lance a mann has set on the side of his set-
tle-down. Armed, she races for her true target.
Heat, wind, time, all are pounding down on her.
She makes her legs stretch, extends her girth.
The Desegator has reached the Snakeel. The
Vultawk reaches the Desegator, banks in a
breakneck swoop.

She reaches first.

The bird drops on her. Its talons scrabble for
a grip, scrapping about her knees. She breathes
through her mouth to keep its rancid carrion
stench from harassing her nose. Its wings beat,
beat, then still. Down her arms runs a red river,
trailing from the butt of the lance from a hole in

the Vultawk's chest. Its own weight had brought its end, as 'though death had hammered it against her ready and waiting nail.

She throws the stiff bird away with all her strength. Behind her the Desegator has finished chowing, and has its head cocked wondering when she'd gotten beside it and why.

"Come, Desegator."

It complies, clamoring up her arm, over her collarbone and into its hidey-hole. With luck it was content 'nough to stay.

Glasga heads for her settle room. She'll reacquaint her vials to her sack-it, collect her sample from the least disturbed part of this town, and skedaddle. She and her little friend aren't welcome. A shout halts her, the same mann from earlier.

"Having a Desegator on your person is dangerous!"

"It is young and can't use its poison."

"What of when it ages?"

"When it ages, so will have I and 'haps I'll be the wiser of its behavior patterns. It is fear or hunger or pain that makes animals strike and this Desegator has no hindrances. Wish I could say the same."

The mann gets her drift and drops away.

#

Glasga has dug further than needed, relishing the grit against her fingertips. The sand is plastered onto itself, caked cool clay. If she didn't know what she knew about water lying on its insides, deep underground, she'd have thought the sand was bleeding, painting her hands in blood. She feels a phantom pain as though she's been cut, but the pain isn't singing from her sore finger joints. What are the chances that this bed is it, the home of the magic she's been seeking, decade on half-decade? Her Desegator leaps into her hole before she can reach in and collect.

"What is it you're up to? You better get back where you belong before another bird snatches you up."

Rather than heeding her warning, the Desegator scraps at the floor of her hole, birthing a little mound which it laps up. Glasga is wondering at how the little reptile scarfs everything down when it starts to glow. It's painful to look at, shaming the sun's brilliance.

"What's coming on? An explosion?

"You traveled far on the wings of a dream. What was it you sought?"

The voice that tickles her ears is mindboggling, a blend of storm roar and wind chimes, gentle and harsh. She can't determine if it's on the air or floating in her mind, but she can tell one thing; it's spilling out of her Desegator.

Somehow that tidbit of fact explains why the voice is so slippery, sounding neither male nor female; Desegators have no gender, rumor has it. Babies sprouted from broken limbs of their fallen, tails or legs growing all-new bodies. Seemed hers had grown some random soul. Unless . . .

"The sand . . . You're talking to me 'cause of the sand, right, little friend? I want my papan. I want you to return my papan."

"I return what is lost."

"He's lost, been gone fifteen years."

"But is he missing or merely missed."

"You can bring him back, know you can. I've been depending on this for years. If you don't return him for me, do it for my little home place 'cause I may have been outcast, but he suited everyone and a thousand little wishes have gotta equal something greater than one."

"You didn't lose but a father, you lost a friend. And you have been handed a new one, loyal to you now, in maturity and centuries thereafter. Still, I'm not against dealing you one more favor."

Through misted eyes, Glasga watches her Desegator slink from the hole and find a place beside her. It blinks once a minute at her and a part of her wants to scoop the little thing up in a chummy squeeze; another part wants to kick the piteous thing sky-high. Her stomach rolls and she has to swallow continuously to keep from heaving.

"If you aren't going to give me my papan, I don't think you can deal me anything. It's all I wanted."

"There is something else you've wanted."

The Desegator glows again, not as sunshiny this time but still painful. Glasga looks away a moment and returns her eyes on a plaque at the reptile's feet, a flat wooden fixture that is a spitting image to the kind birthed by her father's hands.

She snatches it up, turns it over and over, coming to recognize it. It's the welcome her maman kept before her settle-down, a cut-out of an old woman clad in wear similar to Glasga's own, a woman worn and weary by the trench-worthy wrinkles covering her skin, but looking hopeful, hand shielding her eyes as she gazes into the far-off distance. Glasga once sat mes-merized by this creation, her most treasured of her papan's design. She wanted to be that woman, walking and walking on till her aged bones couldn't carry her no more, sun's rays kissing her, wind holding her up, pushing her on.

"You believed you were following your sire's ghost. Instead you were following your own path; one you laid the tracks down for at age four. What you lost was your resolve to see the world and change it with every step. See your sire in the eyes of the opposed and know he's with you for every soul you lift."

The wind blows mighty and then after . . .

"Chirrup. Chi-chi."

"Lost your voice I see. You got me wondering if the sand gave you words or if you conjured 'em on your own, that or I'm getting loopy."

The Desegator takes to Glasga's clothing and she allows it. Mind aflutter, she collects her sand sample before she can forget, the magic sand, not unlike all others once under her fingernails. The plaque her Desegator had given her rests beside her. She plugs her vial and grabs it up.

Glasga is about ready to leave town, stocking her sack-it on the go, when a cry stops her. On the outskirts is a gal not mite older or younger than she is. She's on knees sobbing over a large sack-it done toppled and started belching out some white pellets, what Glasga gathers is food. Seems the gal had too much to carry, and not just in her arms. Some lookers-on men sneer at her while fellow gals shake their heads, pitying, all letting their judgments weigh on her like brick. Glasga parades over, yanks the gal to standing and shoves the plaque into her hands.

"Don't stay tied down. You have working legs and able feet. Walk, no run, and find yourself, see how much you're capable of."

Glasga leaves the young gal, not a glance back though, 'haps, she can relish in an aura eased from black to blue, limitless as open sky. Her hands burn from loss of the wood structure so like those of her papan's making. Yet, she's sure she won't need it, wherever she's going, another item snatching space from her sack-it. Her empty vials sing as they clank against each other, Desegator snores harmonizing.

Glasga studies the distance ahead and smiles.

Sand is calling her.

END

Wendigo Problems
by K.B. Spangler

As far as Breaches go, the one at Kuujjuaq is tiny. It's barely large enough for a gnat to pass through, which is lucky for us: demons are only immortal if you're looking at them through mortal eyes, and a gnat-sized demon lives maybe a couple of years before it crumples up and dies like any other bug.

Also, Kuujjuaq is cold. Balls-creeping *frigid*. I've asked the science team if the subarctic climate has any effect on a demon's lifespan; they say yeah, probably, and it makes them less likely to consider us as a viable vacation spot. So we've got that going for us.

But every couple of decades or so, a warm front moves in, and then we're neck-deep in Wendigos.

You know how you kill a Wendigo?

Iron. Fire. Salt. Soil.

You know how you train someone to kill a Wendigo?

You don't.

Rephrase: you can't. But sometimes you get lucky.

I toss my cigarette on what used to be a high school student, and the body goes up in a cloud of oily smoke. The beast is dead—past dead—but the squealing sound of its burning fur is like one side of a sick conversation.

Fagan has decided that my old SUV is as close as he's going to get to crawling under the covers. He's in the back seat, a shotgun aimed at the windows. I'm not going anywhere near that inevitable accident, so I take out my phone and text him instead.

A long five minutes passes. Long enough for me to finish another cigarette and pull out my bag of rock salt. Then comes the slow squeak of my car's window as Fagan cranks it down.

"Jack?"

I'm barely able to hear him over the summer crickets, which is saying something mighty.

"Yeah." I dump more salt over the corpse. It's still dead and burning, but that's never a sure thing.

"Can I come out?"

"There's another one out here somewhere," I reply. "So. Can you?"

Silence. Then, the unexpected sound of old hinges that have gone past the need for oil, followed by footsteps. The sharp scent of gunmetal shouldn't be enough to cut through the fumes coming from the body, but Fagan is holding the shotgun too close to my face. I push the barrel aside and offer him a cigarette.

"Gave it up."

"Start again," I say, and hand him my lighter. It's a silver Zippo, easily sixty years old. My name used to be engraved along one side until my thumb wore the letters away. I keep it primed and good to go, and it's never let me down, not once. "Kills the smell."

Fagan's face lights up from below. I keep thinking he's younger than he is. He's closer to thirty than twenty, his face scarred from his time in the service. His hands shake as he takes a pull on the cigarette, and then he spends a few minutes coughing until his body remembers the smoke.

I throw another handful of salt on the body. Sparks go up. The monster stays down.

A good night, so far.

Fagan manages to look anywhere except the body. "There's no way that thing was a kid," he finally says.

"Your unit took down a basilisk when you were with Task Force Arrowhead," I say. "Thought you knew your monsters."

"Cockatrice," he snaps. "Not a basilisk. It started out as a fuckin' *chicken,* Jack!"

"And this was a high school student," I say as I nod at the ground beside us. "Do me a favor and stick it with the spear again."

The lance lay where Fagan had dropped it. Truth be told, it wasn't much of a spear. Wendigos come at you like a hurricane, and a man can't stand against that. Best to brace the butt of a sharpened iron lance against a rock or a tree, and let the planet do the heavy lifting instead.

Before Fagan can reach the lance, the fire pops. Bones begin to crack as the last of the marrow boils away. He turns and runs back to the car. I hear him retch on the way.

I toss a last handful of salt into the fire, and go to retrieve the lance.

The blood burns off its tip as I prod the corpse. Fagan had stood his ground when it mattered, and that's all I could ask from him.

The body is finally past the point where it could rise. I use the lance to crush its skull, and push the pieces around until they've become part of the earth.

I send another text to Fagan: *One down, one to go. Headed out. Back before dawn.*

I stomp out what's left of the fire and turn over the soil beneath the ash. It doesn't take too long. Say what you want about monsters, they burn damned fast. Then, about ten seconds before I give up and leave, I hear the car door open again.

Footsteps, hard in military boots, and Fagan joins me by the fire.

He's still got the shotgun, but now he's carrying a second bag of salt.

We head east, towards the wild marshes of Nunavik.

She's left a trail through the woods that a child could follow, so we avoid that and keep a fifty-meter distance between us and the broken underbrush. Fagan turns out to be a pretty good tracker: he finds a spot where she's doubled back around and gone up the hillside.

"Where's she going?" he asks with barely a whisper, just loud enough to register in the range of human hearing. The government trains them well.

"She's hunting," I say, and I turn us back the way we came.

"Sometimes they get a full set of instincts," I explain, once we're a decent distance down the trail and out of earshot. "I think she's one of those. Comes through the change knowing how the woods work, and gets smarter each time she eats."

Fagan mutters an atheist's prayer, all curses and foxholes.

I nod. "Can't sneak up on her, not when she's got the high ground and the wind's blowing towards her."

"Bring her down to us?"

"Yeah."

We reach the car. I've got a cadaver's leg stashed in a cooler, as fresh and bloody as I could find. We carry it between us; Fagan's lashed a plastic strap around its ankle to serve as a handle, and I've got my fingers deep in its meat.

"Is that safe?" he asks, as the car's headlights show reddish trails running down my hand.

"For me? Yeah," I tell him. "I've been doing this a long, long time."

We set up a portable stand in a pair of black spruce, the leg dangling over a snare trap. Fagan tells me that no self-respecting predator would fall for such an obvious setup; I remind him that this is no bear.

"She's been cursed," I say, as I wipe my bloody hand on my jeans. "They're compelled. Once they know there's human flesh around, they can't stop until they've eaten. The young ones are usually dumb about it, and relentless."

That takes a moment to sink in. Once it does, Fagan glares at me.

I shrug. "We killed her mate. She was already after us."

Fagan and I settle down in the stand to wait. He tells me about the cockatrice, and the Breach near Andover. "Beautiful place," he says. "Like here. Woods, not a lot of people."

"They know," I say, as I point my nose towards Kuujjuaq. It's twenty kilometers away, but there's still a murmur of machines in the air. "They know, and they try to stay away from the dark places. Mostly."

"There's an old mill at Andover," Fagan says. "This guy I met over there? He was British SAS— he told me an actual wizard closed the Breach back in the Middle Ages. They built the mill over it to keep the seal closed."

"What happened?" I see a flock of ptarmigan take to the night sky: she's circling, getting closer.

"Bunch of cultists tried to reopen it. Blew up the mill in 2002. The Brits got it resealed, and rebuilt the mill on top, but..."

"Cockatrice problems."

"Yeah."

We're quiet for a while. I listen; Fagan's got a strong heart, and its drumbeat drowns out any sounds of the beast in the brush.

"Anybody try to close your Breach?" he asks.

I nod before I remember that he can't see me. "Can't find it," I say. "It's too small. Besides, nothing crosses over except bugs. Kuujjuaq ain't nobody's priority."

"They say that's what happened in Andover," he tells me. "Insect-sized demon slips through a crack, infects a chicken. Two, three months later, it's a cockatrice."

"Same thing here," I say. "Except with humans."

Fagan unbuttons a flap on his jacket and pulls out a black tube. A night scope: it hums as he turns it on and peers into the forest.

"You won't see her," I tell him. "She's part of the woods now."

"Caught her boyfriend easy enough."

"He was ..." I grope around for the right word. "... unfinished."

He scans the forest until he's satisfied. The tube stops humming and goes back into his pocket. He's slow and quiet for another hour, all conversation going on in his head as we wait.

The sky loses its stars and goes gray.

"Do they sleep?" he asks.

"They get something like sleep," I say. "They have a den and hole up during the day. They close their eyes. But they don't slow down, and they're twice as mean once cornered."

"You can't trap them in their den?"

"I've tried," I reply. "Chased them inside, and threw fire after them. Never ends well. They need to be broken before they can burn."

"Grenades?" That military mind of his is ticking. "Maybe bury some landmines..."

"Happy to try again," I said. "Got any landmines on you?"

Not on him, no, but in town was a storage unit full of equipment the Canadian Armed Forces had provided for their intrepid young Wendigo hunter. We pull down the stand and the cadaver leg, and walk back to my SUV.

She kept pace with us the whole trip, tracking us through the trees. As we drove away, she howled loud enough for Fagan to hear, and the smell of his fear rose within the car.

Kuujjuaq's a nice enough place, if all you need to get by is coffee and cold. I don't go there much. I've got a little cabin outside of town. I hunt for myself, mostly, and Amazon and my post office box set me up for anything else. Twice a year, a man from Ottawa flies out to see if I'm still alive. He always brings money: someone's decided I deserve a salary.

This new government *pays* me to hunt monsters. I'll laugh and cry about this until my dying day.

Food before firearms. I point Fagan towards the only diner in town. As we go inside, tired faces turn towards us. Beside the door is a bulletin board, plastered in layers of old paper. Near the top are flyers with black-and-white photos of the missing.

I take down the one of a boy in a hockey jersey.

A woman sobs and leaves. Everyone else falls about in relief.

A waitress with the high color of the Naskapi brings us two mugs and a carafe half-full of hot coffee. "Thank you, Mr. Fiddler," she tells me.

I nod at Fagan. "He's a natural," I tell her.

She smiles at him, her eyes a little warmer than when she looks at me. She rests a hand on his shoulder. "Thank God," she says, and walks away.

He finishes his coffee before saying, "She meant that."

"Yeah." I point to the crucifix over the diner's front door. "Big believers up here."

"You?"

"Hard not to be," I admit. "They've got answers, and this life doesn't offer too many of those. I love their version of the soul, too, like a tiny second self inside of you, and any choice you make can help or hurt them both. But I'm none too easy with what they did to my people."

"You're Naskapi?"

"Oji-Cree. We live down near the Lakes. I'm up here because..." I tap my fingers on the photograph of the boy.

Fagan turns the flyer towards him. He studies the boy's face, and his pulse rises a little, but all he says is, "Real shame."

The poster for the kid's girlfriend is still hanging by the door. I get up and retrieve it, bringing the thumbtack along so I remember to put it up again on our way out. I slide the flyer across the table to Fagan.

He pretends to watch something happening that only he can see. I wait him out. Eventually, his eyes drop and he can't help but read the flyer.

"Seventeen," he says. "An art student. And barely seventeen."

"There's plenty of taboos against going into these woods," I tell him. "But if you're seventeen and looking for a place to fuck without getting caught, taboos can work for you."

He starts to laugh. "Oh, no," he says. "Oh *no!*
Tell me I'm wrong—tell me they killed and ate
some poor hiker to catalyze the curse."

"Nope." I shake my head. "Once those demons infect you, catalysis is easy. Chew your
nails, bite your own tongue—"

"Or go down on your girlfriend," he says,
rubbing his face with his hands.

"Happens all the time," I tell him. The food
arrives: his pancakes thick and swimming in
butter; my omelet mostly meats with another
side of meat. We shut up until the waitress finishes another round of smiling at Fagan and
leaves. Then, I pick up where we left off. "It's a
warm spring. A demon comes through, infects a
couple of kids getting it on..."

"I've been wondering about that," he says,
digging into the pancakes with the enthusiasm
of a man who has expended several thousand
calories in a pitched battle against a monster.

"The briefing said most Wendigos show up in the dead of winter."

"That's the thing," I tell him. "They don't start out like what you saw. The curse might grab your mind, but until you take a human life for the purpose of eating the body, it won't grab your soul.

"Starts small," I continue around bites of bacon. "The craving. You barely notice it those first few weeks. You think you're just extra horny, maybe, or you pick up the habit of gnawing on the inside of your cheek.

"Maybe you let it get so bad you start graverobbing. That's okay. Nobody's using that body anymore, so you're just a ghoul. Nasty, yeah, but not a danger. You can sleep in your own bed at night."

Fagan's head snaps up. He looks around the diner, at the people chatting and smiling, and then back to me.

I nod.

He shudders.

"Can't be helped, not living around here. Just something we deal with. Maybe one in fifty are infected, but we know to watch each other pretty close, just in case.

"And there's me," I add. "If you know you can't control it, if you *know* things are about to go bad ... you know where I live.

"But say you and your girlfriend are just kids. You got no real self-control yet," I say, pointing my fork at the flyers. "You get infected, give into the cravings. Or maybe you can't stomach grave-robbing, but killing a hiker? That's fine by you. Once that hiker's soul enters your system, you lose your own.

"The fangs come first," I say. "All the better to eat you with, right? If they keep killing, their bodies start to change. They twist all tall and lanky, nothing but bones. By the time there's frost on the ground, they've gone full-blown Wendigo, fur, claws, and all.

"But," I say, as I wave the waitress over for more coffee. "If you're strong enough, you'll take those cravings and shove them down. They're an itch in your system. Nothing more, unless..."

"...unless you and your family get snowed in during a bad winter," Fagan finishes. "And there's nothing to eat."

The waitress's hand shakes a little as she finishes topping off my cup. This time, she hurries away without flirting with Fagan.

We're not asked to pay; Fagan leaves the cost of our meals, plus a big tip. I return the flyer of the art student to the bulletin board, the thumbtack going back in its hole.

Then Fagan takes me to his storage unit.

It takes me a while to remember to shut my mouth.

"You expecting a *war?*" I finally ask.

"Close. This isn't here for me," Fagan says, as he squeezes past black plastic crates filled with more weaponry than I've ever seen outside of a movie. "This is all for you, for you to train me and whoever comes after me. Once I'm up to speed, they're gonna reassign me five hundred kilometers away, and one who comes after me will get reassigned five hundred kilometers in another direction..." As he talks, he's lifting crates and covers, showing off bazookas and missiles and things I can't put a name to but smell like cold metal death.

"*Why?!*" is all I can think to ask.

"Climate change," he says, as he hands me a shotgun's bigger, meaner brother. "Those damned bugs are covering more ground before they freeze 'n' die. It's not too bad today, but twenty? Thirty years from now?" He places a case of landmines on top of the nearest crate. "Gotta be proactive, man. Said so yourself—that's the only way to handle Wendigos."

"Why the fuck didn't you show me all of this before I took you hunting?"

"Needed to see how you do it old-school," he says. "They told me you know everything there is to know about killing these things. Sometimes the old ways are best.

"Or," he adds, with a thrust of a knife to a rather tall space of empty air, "can be improved."

I get myself moving. I don't recognize most of what's in the storage unit, so I grab as many user manuals as I can find, a little light reading to learn what the Canadian Armed Forces has managed to sidle into my possession. Fagan talks me through the gear he thinks will work for fighting a Wendigo in her den. Classic pineapple grenades, with their cast-iron shells; we pull the pin, throw, and run. Flechette sabot ammunition for those mutant shotguns, in case the grenades don't work. Antipersonnel mines, in case she comes after us in a red rage and forgets to watch her feet.

We load up my SUV with enough arms and armor to take out Kuujjuaq, or maybe Montreal, and drive out to where we left the boy in ashes. We've got iron, fire, and salt in spades; the earth always provides itself, and I don't think the Department of National Defence can improve on that.

My lance rides on top of the pile.

When we reach the burned-out body, I tell Fagan to stay in the car so his too-strong heart doesn't drum out what I need to hear. I walk a kilometer or so through the woods, hearing nothing, smelling nothing ... That doesn't mean she's gone, mind, or even gone to bed. It just means she's good.

I return to the car to get Fagan, and we set out to find her den.

We walk in silent circles for most of the morning. At noon, I catch her scent, and guide us to the edge of the Koksoak River. There's a timber fall down a shallow slope; she's nesting in a tangle of water-broken trees.

We scout the routes: nope. If she had denned in a cave, there'd be one way in and one way out—I've never met a Wendigo that could claw its way through solid rock. Wood is a whole other story. Catching her by surprise won't work, either: if we try to get close, she'll hear us coming as we rattle our way over the dry branches.

Fagan and I backtrack, getting most of the way to the car, before he says, "There's a rocket launcher back in town."

"Hmm." Worth considering. Shoot a rocket into the timber and let the explosion flush her out...

Except the river runs straight through the center of town.

I tell Fagan no, we can do better than risk setting an enraged Wendigo on the good folks of Kuujjuaq, especially if she's injured and on fire besides. We go north again, to a little place I know, a hollow at the end of an old timber road.

It smells of campfires and beer: the local kids sneak out here on the weekends.

Fagan curses as he takes in the signs of teenage habitation. "Sorry, Jack, but your taboos aren't doing *shit*."

The hollow is nestled against the side of a cliff, and screams of human beings. I've used it as a box trap for Wendigos before. Not recently, and I hope it's been long enough: I can't smell death here anymore, but she might.

I text a few friends in town, tell them put out the word to lock up the teenagers for the night, and Fagan and I get to work. It takes us a few round trips to the car to bring all of our gear. A storm's moving in, fast and heavy, and we set up what we can before the sky breaks apart.

There's a rusted-out husk of a logging truck at the back of the hollow. Fagan and I make a damp camp under its leaking roof. I can't hear or smell anything with the rain drumming down, and the lightning plays hell with my night vision, so I ask Fagan to pull out his shiny night scope and keep an eye on the road.

"Can-*not* believe you let the kids come here," he mutters.

"Sex and drugs beat cannibalism, every time. The infection rate's too low to make the threat stick."

His focus doesn't leave the road, but I'm pretty sure that if he wasn't a stone-cold military man, he'd be rolling his eyes.

"Taboos only work if you believe in them," I add. "Kids don't believe in much except themselves."

"That's fair," he mutters.

The rain keeps coming. Lightning strikes a nearby tree; Fagan hisses as his night scope hits him in one eye with all the bright it can throw at him. I pull the collar on my old leather coat up, tuck my hat down, and take my turn keeping watch over the cadaver's leg we strung up in the middle of the hollow.

It's too windy. The leg wobbles back and forth on its line, a piece of a person still kicking on its own. It's a type of gory I haven't seen before, and watching it is beginning to turn my stomach.

I start talking.

"Ever study anthropology?"

Not the best way to start this particular conversation, maybe, but I've yet to find a better one. Fagan doesn't miss much. I'd rather lay this out where he can see it than have him trip over it in the dark.

"What?" he says. "No."

"You should start. It's like smoking—it goes along with this job. I told this scientist once, he should go and make a map of where cannibalism is practiced, and where it's forbidden. I told him we could chart what comes out of a Breach based on what the locals do to survive."

"I'd like to think that cannibalism is a big universal *no*," Fagan says.

"Human nature doesn't work that way," I say. "While back, I needed to lay low. Decided to go south. Folks in the north, we've got Wendigos, so our taboos? We don't eat people. Ever. But down south, there's this noisy rumor that eating a fallen enemy gives you strength.

"I kept asking around as I went, down through the States and past them. Kept hearing the same rumors from a hundred different kinds of people, that you should eat the heart or the liver of your enemies. You do that, you take on their powers. But it's got to be a righteous victory—the enemy has to have been defeated in noble combat—otherwise, you're just another monster.

"And me, since I know Wendigos, and I know that they get stronger each time they eat, I'm thinking there's a different side of the curse at work. Kin to the Wendigo one, maybe, where cold murder makes you lose your soul. But if you win some of your enemy's powers in a battle?

Well, maybe that's not so much a curse as much as it's putting some balance back into the world—"

Fagan's hand goes up in a fist.

I close my stupid mouth and start to listen. There's an undertone to the storm, a *hsss-hsss-hsss* that doesn't sound like any rain I've heard before.

I throw Fagan from the truck as the beast dives through its roof.

She comes in with her claws out, razor-sharp and ripping through metal to find my throat. The rusted steel leaves deep cuts along her arms, and her fur turns crimson. She tears out a decent-sized piece of my neck, and it's down her gullet before I can do anything about it.

More claws and teeth, but now I'm fighting back, turning the truck against her. My throat's already halfway to normal but she can't come back from the sharp edges of the steel as quick. I'm laying into her with everything I've got, but what I've got is an old pinion shaft as a sword and a slab of the truck's roof as a shield, and neither of these are cold iron.

A grenade flies into the truck and bounces off my shield, and I'm cursing out Fagan in every language I know as I hurl myself through the hole where a window used to be.

The truck goes up in a bright red cloud.

She's howling now, one arm gone, but she's just eaten so it rebuilds itself in a spiral of wet magics. I shout at Fagan to run—she'll be twice as hungry after that—but my throat's not fully knit and my voice is a frog's croak. She comes at me, twelve feet tall and roaring.

The truck is burning, so I turn into the flames.

Somehow she knows where we buried the landmines. The ground around the truck is a kill zone she crosses like a dancer, long legs and clawed feet finding the safe spaces between the mines.

She keeps coming, straight through the fire, a demon grown from a young woman's flesh.

More claws across my back. Leather rips. Something breaks, and my legs stop working. I'm thinking I might be done.

Hey, I had a long run.

I drag myself from the truck and fall in a useless heap onto the soggy earth. She stands over me, teeth barred and panting.

"Good fight," I gasp.

Half of her head disappears.

Fagan throws me my lance. My spine's nowhere near healed, but there's no trick to doing what I've done a thousand times before: I sink the handle into the ground, and point the sharpened tip at her chest.

The second blast from the shotgun knocks her forward. All I have to do is hold the lance steady.

There's not much light left in her remaining eye, but there's enough to make us worry. Fagan shoulders her body into the truck, and sets out to grab what we brought to keep the fire going.

When he returns with kindling and three gallons of kerosene, I'm able to walk again. He finds me kneeling beside her body, a hunting knife in one hand and her heart in the other.

"Jack, what the hell?!" Fagan swears. "You didn't do this last night."

"He didn't earn it," I say, and place her heart into the small cooler that had held the cadaver's leg, now rinsed clean by the rain. "He was just an unlucky kid. She was a monster."

Fagan's eyes go wide as his brain runs a marathon. He picks up my ruined jacket and sees the slashes across the back, with too much blood around them.

"Oh," he says, and his knees give out so he sits down hard in the rain and the mud. "Oh."

"It's not for me," I tell him. "Stick around for a few more hunts. If you decide you're in this for the long haul, I'll cook you dinner."

END

A Day in the Life
by Robin M Black

"Make sure you don't over-brown the mushrooms. And the sauce should be a caramel color, if you're sure to whisk it counterclockwise while turning your wrist."

Jeremiah Butler raised an eyebrow and tucked the pen and notepad into his pocket without writing anything down. The customer's bland smile set the muscle under his eye twitching. "Sir, if you mean to imply that I am unable to cook a simple mushroom béchamel, then I would inquire as to why you've shown up in my restaurant at all."

The customer's face fell, his cheeks turning a splotchy mixture of red and pink. "Oh no, Mr. Butler, I never meant to—I just have particular tastes and I—"

"Yes, sir. Your meal will be at your table momentarily."

The man, done up in his finest business suit, looked a colorful cross between embarrassed and indignant in the face of his even finer-dressed friends. He slumped just a fraction in his seat.

Jeremiah had just turned back to the comforts of his kitchen when the restaurant door creaked open. A chill permeated the air that he knew only he felt.

He glared over his shoulder at the dark-haired woman who now stormed through his tables. No one else was the least bit disturbed; not even when she passed through a woman's white cheddar polenta and garlicky greens, the customer's half poised fork spearing the newcomer right through the chest.

He didn't have time for this today. He had orders to fill and inventory to check and paychecks to calculate and a dozen other things to do. But he knew all too well that the dead could be quite unsympathetic to the schedules of the living. Why would this woman be any different?

He stomped to the kitchen, glad for the free-swinging doors that were impossible to slam. He waited until the dish-boy had started clinking around plates and skillets and pots before he turned to face the woman tapping her sneakered foot at his station.

"Oh, Jeremiah, I just recently died and there's a horrible, evil person I need to get rid of before I can move on! All the other ghosts said to come straight to you, that you're the best!" He said in a sing-song voice as he sliced

mushrooms, not looking at her. "Oh, well, I'm glad you've found me so easily. I'm a bit busy right now, could you come sometime when I'm not at work?"

She opened her mouth to speak, but he held up a hand. "*Oh no, Jeremiah. That would be too convenient and thoughtful of a ghost. I must demand your time and attention now, because I'm different!*"

"I'll have you know that I—"

"Are a special case? It's an emergency? He's bent on destroying the earth? He cheated on you and ten other women? He has kittens tied up in bags?" Jeremiah ticked off possibilities on his fingers. "Or is he actually not a he? Some other gender plaguing you today?"

"Are you always such an ass to the dead?" She frowned at him, hands on her hips.

She looked pretty healthy for someone who was dead. Her hair black was tied up in a messy bun. Her lips were still red from lipstick, and her green eyes were wide and clear. She would have almost looked like a true person if not for the slight fade to her skin, the way the light didn't bend around her correctly, but passed through her, like dirty air. There were also the dark, dusty purple bruises blossoming around her neck, still forming perfect fingertips and thumbprints.

"I don't like wasting time," he said. "Like to get to business. Who do you want dead, and who are you going to trade for them?"

"I just want one person dead. And I'm not trading anybody."

Jeremiah shook his head. "Not how it works. I kill whoever you want dead, and you give me someone else to kill who fits my profile."

"This isn't a dating site, it's murder." The woman laughed and leaned onto his counter. "And you're putting too much nutmeg in your béchamel."

"If one more person tells me how to do my job, I'm going to—"

"Kill someone?" The woman snorted. "That's the goal then, isn't it?"

Jeremiah grumbled. "First the man wants brown béchamel, now a ghost thinks she can tell me how to kill people. Today is just not a good day."

"Hey, my name's not Ghost. My name is Katie, and you better learn it if you're supposed to be working with me." Katie sat herself on his counter, her legs and butt not disturbing the flour sack there at all, even as it went right through her thighs. "I promise I've got a sweet pot."

"What does that even mean? Were you a card dealer or something?" He glanced over her sneakers swinging through the lower cabinets and her tattered jeans. She didn't look like a card dealer, even off the clock.

"Nope. Construction worker. And it doesn't matter." She shook her head again, sending her bangs into a wild frenzy. "I got someone you're gonna want to meet."

"What'd he do?"

"Oh, the usual thing. Cashing his worker's paychecks, underpaying them, threatening them if they went to the law. True scumbag, he is."

"Threatening what?" Jeremiah dumped the freshly sautéed mushrooms in with his white sauce, watching it carefully. He'd be damned if he was going to burn his sauce just because some jack cracked open a cookbook once ten years ago and thought he knew how to cook. Old white dudes were always trying to tell young black chefs how to cook their food. It was the most annoying part of his day.

"Depends on the worker. For immigrants, it's deportation. For the homeless, it's turning them in to the government as frauds. He's got a list of how and who he can control."

"Sounds like a regular Santa Claus." Jeremiah nodded and poured his sauce over thin noodles, twisting them into a ball on the plate. He wiped the excess away. "So, like you said, that's the usual in the business owner fare I work with. What makes this guy stand out?"

"I'm not the first person he's murdered." Katie tried to swipe some of the sauce residue in the skillet. She pouted. Her finger had moved straight through it. "Being dead is the worst."

"Who am I to argue? Never died before." He set a twig of thyme over the top and stood back to examine his work. "So he makes a habit of killing people then?"

"Yeah, not to make you feel like a hypocrite. But he's got quite a stash of trophies from his older victims." Katie watched the plate, fingers thrumming on the counter. She had so much movement and didn't make any noise. "He's quite fond of hunting the homeless."

Jeremiah nodded and ran his hands over his apron. "Well, if it makes me a hypocrite, then so be it. I've been homeless, I empathize. And two for one deals don't come along often. It'll be nice to be home in the morning."

"That's the spirit!" She leaned back and giggled as Jeremiah set the pasta on the pass. He signaled to his co-lead that he was stepping out. He was thankful that kitchens were loud. No one had heard him talking to Katie.

Stepping into the alley was like moving from a hell of hot steam and screeching workers into a cool, dark hole that smelled like garbage. Jeremiah flipped out his phone and pounded the one button. He nodded when it rang and pulled a cigarette from his apron pocket. He fumbled with his lighter, nearly dropped his phone.

Katie watched him from beside the door, arms crossed. He scowled at her and tapped his phone, shooing her away with his smoking hand.

He'd just gotten his cigarette lit, the blue smoke curling from between his fingers, when there was the beep of someone pushing the answer button too many times.

"Yes? Wha'? Whozit?" Jeremiah's heart thumped heavy at Morgan's sleep heavy Belfast accent.

"Come on, love, you know only one person ever calls you." Jeremiah flicked ash and chuckled. "Have you been asleep all day?"

"You know how it is. Graveyard shift keeps me from missing you. What's up?" Morgan yawned. He was fighting off more sleep.

"I'll be out late tonight, I'm afraid. I've got a two for one deal, so it'll be quick."

Morgan whined on the other end of the line.

"Marrying a ghost whisperer was my worst life choice yet." Morgan mumbled. "Be glad I love you and have no common sense."

"Wouldn't have it any other way. Now, get back to sleep. I'll be back before you know it."

"Better be, or I'll be off at work and you'll be home alone." Morgan's voice dropped. "Never get to see you anymore."

He was getting close to losing Morgan to sleep again. "Yeah, yeah. Go on then, back to dreamland for you. Love you, babe."

"Love you, too. You owe me."

"I'll keep it in mind." Jeremiah hung up, grinning despite the long shift and longer night ahead.

"Someone looks like a teenager in love." Katie leaned through the wall of his kitchen, green eyes wide. "That was adorable. You should call him again."

"Look here, we're not friends. You can't just listen in on my phone calls. A man needs privacy." Jeremiah smooshed his cigarette down to a nub on his palm and flicked it to the garbage can. "Get over here and tell me what I need to know before I go haul off and try to kill this man. You better tell me if he's some hulk man or something," he said, heading back into the kitchen.

Katie snorted. "Hardly."

It turned out that Katie knew far more about her ex-boss than most of his past ghosts knew about their targets. She knew where he lived, when he slept and ate, how often he left the house, his lack of self-defense training, and what he'd do when Jeremiah showed up.

Jeremiah finished up his last plate of Swiss chard and ricotta ravioli, tossed in lemon brown butter sauce, just as Katie finished speaking, hands folded on her lap and cheeks flushed a dull pink.

"So I take it you two weren't always worst enemies." Jeremiah tilted his head at her as he placed his dish on the pass and wiped his hands on his apron. "That's a lot of information about a guy you claim to hate."

"We dated a month or so. He seemed nice at first, and I was new to the job." She picked at her nail, not looking at him. "After a while, he kept doing creepy stuff. Got crazy jealous. The guy was the world's worst boyfriend. I'd gone by his place to tell him to stop leaving flowers in my car when I caught him threatening Huerta."

"Must be a real piece of work. Well, let's get this place closed up and head out. No point in waiting all night."

Katie was quiet through the process of closing up. He turned to her as he locked up the door, waving off his dish-boy and co-lead. "If you're having second thoughts, you don't have to come. You just have to clean up when I'm done."

"I can't touch anything." She demonstrated by trying to move a chair. "See, nothing. How am I supposed to clean?"

"You'll figure it out when you get there. There are some perks to being a ghost. Or so I've been told. Are you coming or not?" He unlocked his car, sliding into the smooth faux leather seats.

"No, I'm coming. I was just thinking." She slid in beside him, crossing her long legs and slumping. "Do you imagine you're some kind of vigilante? Some kind of unsung hero? Or do you just do this for the hell of it?"

"Look, I've been killing folks for ghosts since I was fifteen. I don't pretend to be anyone special. Ghosts want people dead, I want people safe. We work together, we accomplish our goals. What's better than that?" The engine roared to life and he sighed in the cool air from his ac. "I don't imagine heroes kill people."

"I guess not." Katie shrugged. "Just wondering who I was dealing with."

"No problem. Now, you said 195 Brooks Road?" He asked. Katie nodded. "Alright, let's go."

195 Brooks Road could have fit Jeremiah's apartment in it two times and still had room left over. Jeremiah didn't consider himself rich, but he was well off. This man's house was beyond well off. The grass was green and full even in the middle of fall, and he counted fourteen miniature rose bushes lining the extended driveway. He grimaced at the fancy embossed lettering that proudly proclaimed the homeowner as *Winner of Best Lawn, three years and counting!* Only rich people cared about stuff like that.

"Yeah, I know. Piece of work, isn't he?" Katie mumbled, trying to kick the sign over. It didn't move.

"Alright, Katie, is he armed?" Jeremiah poised his hand over the door.

"He has a gun taped under his table because he saw it in a gangster movie. Just stay out of the kitchen."

"Alright then." He knocked a cheery beat on the door.

There was a shuffle and a groan, and a blond-haired man poked his head out. "Whattya want?" Blue eyes blinked out from black fringe, and a scruffy chin jutted out in annoyance. "Who th' hell are you?"

"Hello, I'm here on behalf of Katie..." He stalled, looking at Katie for help.

"Collins," she provided.

"Katie Collins," Jeremiah finished.

The man paused a minute to process the name before he turned to run. Jeremiah didn't know where the man thought he was running to. He shrugged and closed the door behind him, locking it. The kitchen was empty. "Are you sure there aren't any more firearms in the house?"

"Well, there wasn't when I was around." Katie shrugged. "Maybe he's trying to run out back?"

"To a fenced in backyard? Ok." Jeremiah listened for the slam of a screen door. He ran, following Katie to where the door still bounced, and lunged at the scrambling figure on the ground. The man had tripped over his stairs while trying to get his boots on. "Nice to meet you again. That was quite a strong reaction."

"How do you know Katie? Was she after you too? She was mad. Whatever she told you was a lie. I wouldn't trust her." The man spoke too quickly, squirming in Jeremiah's hold.

"You know, I don't like it when you people run. If you run I have to incapacitate you and it's just so much less fun that way." Jeremiah held the man still, breathing deep and calm, until they were breathing together. Then he dropped him, swinging his fist around hard to hit him between the eyes. The man fell like a stone into a pile of crumpled pajamas and scrawny limbs.

"Well, now what? You're not done are you?" Katie leaned down to inspect him. "If so, I want my money back. He's not dead."

"Have patience. It's not like you don't have the rest of forever." Jeremiah dragged the man by his ankles, checking for neighbors peeking over the fence. Luckily, their exchange had been fairly quiet. He hefted the man's legs onto his back, holding him upside down.

He dragged his victim into the house, counting *one, two, three* bumps on the stairs from where the man's head bounced on the ground. Jeremiah searched for something to secure him, duct tape or rope or anything. "What do rich people fix things with?"

"I think they just buy new things." Katie shrugged. "What do you need?"

"Something to keep him from running off while I get my tools."

"He's out cold. I don't think he's going anywhere." Katie tried to poke the man's slack face.

"That will last another minute or so tops. He'll be disoriented, but he'll still try to run." Jeremiah huffed at the kitchen's fluorescent light buzzing overhead and the pile of dirty dishes. "This kitchen is a nightmare."

"You're a nightmare." Katie glanced around and bit her lip. "He has handcuffs in the bedroom. Would that work?"

Jeremiah raised an eyebrow. "I make no judgment on your taste, Katie."

He followed her back to the room. She pointed at a pair of fuzzy handcuffs in purple and pink on the dresser and another pair slung over one of the bedposts in cheetah print. "The fuzzy bits come off, I think."

"Nah. I'll leave them on. He can feel as weird about them as I do." He sauntered back into the room and grabbed a chair from the kitchen. The man groaned and shifted. He sat up just as Jeremiah finished moving the chair into the living room. "Just in time, sleeping beauty. Nice to see you, too."

"Huroo?" The man slurred out, but neither Jeremiah nor Katie understood him.

"I hear you've not been very nice to your workers, sir." Jeremiah lifted him onto the chair, clicking one side of a pair of handcuffs to the man's ankle and the other side to the chair leg. He wrestled the other pair around the man's wrists, putting one arm in the space under the back of the chair and the seat. It left the man twisted in an awkward position. "You give them a job, make them work for cheap. I bet you sleep real fine at night, telling yourself you're doing charity. I bet every time you start dating a nice pretty lady, you pat yourself on the back for being such a remarkable human being."

"I treat my workers well!" The man found his voice, albeit he still sounded weak. "I give them all sorts of benefits they'd never get under anyone else! I'm not the only one who hires illegals!"

"Oh, no, you see, you hire *people.* Do you offer them good dental? Is that it? What is it you think you're giving them that makes up for their pay? For the constant threat you hold over their lives? What makes you think you're excusable?"

"I... I give them phones! I get them phones they can pay off on their paychecks! I let them rent houses and... and I let them call in whenever they like. One of them invites me to his kid's birthday party every year."

"Oh, so you mean you let them pay you money?" Jeremiah laughed. "He who giveth can taketh away. How many different places have you wiggled into in their lives? How dependent have you made them?"

"What do you care? I've never met you a day in my life. You have no proof. No one is going to believe you." The man was screaming at Jeremiah as he walked out the door.

"Oh, do you think I'm leaving? I've barely gotten started." Jeremiah turned to Katie and smiled. The man couldn't see her, but that didn't bother Jeremiah so much. "Katie, let me know if he tries to get away. I'll just be a second."

He jogged out to his car, checking to make sure no one was on the road. He pulled out a set of butcher's knives from the trunk of his car. They were silvery and sharp and gleaming orange in the lamplight. It sent a thrill through him just to hold them again. Morgan would be proud his Christmas gift was put to good use.

He re-entered the house and let out a low whistle. "I'm ba-a-ack. Katie, check out these beauties." He lifted one of the knives out of its wrap, and twirled it.

She grinned. "Don't you own a vegetarian restaurant? That's an impressive cimeter." She ran a finger along the edge and sighed. "And the breaking knife is one of the better ones I've seen. This must be an awfully expensive set. Was it a gift?"

"Yeah, from my husband. How do you know about them?" The man squirmed in the chair, neck swinging wildly around as he searched for Katie.

"Ex-girlfriend worked in a butcher's shop. She was allowed to bring the knives home when they replaced them. She'd have been impressed with these."

"Who are you talking to?" The man said, quickly and out of breath, chest heaving with panic. He started to bellow. "HELP ME! HELP!"

Jeremiah shook his head as the man continued to scream. "If you'd just been quiet, this could have gone much faster. But now you've been loud, and I have to go through the tedium of shutting you up before I get started. I can't enjoy it if you're hollering the whole time."

The man's eyes widened, and he screamed louder for the last time as Jeremiah ripped a strip off of his shirt, and then another. He twisted one up, stuffed it into the man's mouth, and then tied the other one to cover it. The man coughed and gagged around the shirt, but eventually gave up trying to spit it out. He watched Jeremiah turn the knives over and inspect them. He wasn't looking for anything in particular, but the way his victim's face went death-white was too good to pass up.

"We're going to start with the cleaver, move on to the breaking knife, and then, we'll finish up with the boning knife. Don't worry, you won't feel a thing after the first fifteen minutes.

Probably less than that." Jeremiah stepped up, and swung the cleaver down. The first cut was always the most difficult. The man struggled, making the cut uneven. "You're lucky I want to get home to my husband. If I rush through you, I might be able to get a good half hour of cuddling in tonight."

"You are one sick guy, you know that Jeremiah?" Katie covered her mouth, her nose scrunched up in disgust as blood squelched out from the cleaver. "Not sure he quite deserved this."

"Should have been fairer. Don't forget, he murdered you."

"Oh yeah. Forgot I was dead for a second." Katie's hand moved to her chest and she nodded.

True to his word, Jeremiah was done in fifteen minutes. Less than halfway through his work, the man went limp and silent. Jeremiah straightened, grinning as he held a still heart in his hands. "Good work. Haven't lost my touch. It's been almost a month since the last time I did this."

"Any reason you go for the heart?" She grimaced at the pooled blood on the floor.

"Makes sure the job is done. No one lives without a heart." Jeremiah tossed it over his shoulder and looked her in the eyes. "And it's pretty fitting. What kind of heartless bastard does all this anyway?"

"You do this just for the heartless puns, don't you?"

"Wordplay, I believe is what it's called." Jeremiah shrugged. "And yeah. That's part of it."

"So you said I'd know what to do?" Katie looked around at the pooled up blood on the carpet and the corpse. "That's quite a lot of evidence. Do you need to clean up or something?"

"That's your job. Just, light it up. All ghosts can do it. Burn it down, then move on. No worries, ghostly fires are particularly nasty. It'll destroy anything that can be used against me."

"You're a really horrible person, you know?" She looked around. "Do I just concentrate?"

"I don't know, I've never been a ghost. I'd assume so." Jeremiah rubbed the back of his neck, packing up his knives. "If it helps, you can try snapping."

"Thanks, I'll get right on that." Katie stared at her fingertips and squinted. "Thanks a lot, Jeremiah. I'm not sure I could have moved on knowing he was still out there, killing off people."

"Surprised I didn't get him earlier. It's no problem. That's my job. Ghost whisperer, murderous chef." Jeremiah waved and walked out the door, closing it quietly to make sure he didn't attract attention. "I've got ten minutes to get home if I want to see Morgan. I'm off." He waved and jumped into his car.

He sped all the way home, down empty streets and barely lit back roads. Morgan's SUV was still parked in the driveway when he got home. None of the lights were on.

He shed his shirt and pants in the entryway and tossed his bloodied knives into the sink. He'd clean them properly in the morning. Well, later in the morning, when he woke up. He wiggled under the covers and wrapped his arms around Morgan's middle. He buried his head in his husband's back right as the alarm went off.

"You know I have to get up in fifteen minutes, right?" Morgan mumbled over his shoulder, fingers lacing into Jeremiah's.

He groaned. "No, you aren't allowed."

"Yeah, yeah. No complaining. This is cuddle time." Morgan pushed back against him. He was warm and soft against Jeremiah's chest. "You need a bath."

"Shut up." Jeremiah snorted. "You'll be reporting on another arson in a couple of days. There may even be a dead guy in there. Katie didn't know how to do the fire."

Morgan shrugged. "Did you use the cleaver?"

"Yeah."

"Aw, you hurried just for me." Morgan turned in his embrace to face him. "That deserves a kiss."

"Just one?" Jeremiah grinned as Morgan's lips pressed to his.

"Just one."

END

Nahuales

by Anton Rose

The envelope arrived in the early morning, with the sound of birdsong. When Elena found it, she opened the front door and ran out onto the pavement. It was early December in Oxford, and a thin layer of frost coated the small patch of grass at the front of the house. The only sounds were the rumble of a bus on one of the nearby roads and the faint peal of bells from somewhere in the distance, Christ Church or St. Giles. The postman was nowhere to be seen, but Elena's eyes were drawn to a lamppost on the other side of the road. A silver-brown owl perched on top.

Back inside, Elena examined the envelope. The address was handwritten, and whoever wrote it had included both of her middle names, which she rarely used. Inside, she found a plane ticket to Mexico City, a bundle of crinkled pesos, and a printed flyer advertising the year's La Rejunta celebration.

"What's going on?"

Elena's housemate stood at the top of the stairs, wearing an oversized Oxford University sweater.

"I think I'm going home," Elena said.

#

It was a patchwork journey from the airport to Elena's village, involving a bus and then two taxis, because the first one broke down. The second taxi dropped Elena off at the bottom of the village. It sat on a wide, gently-sloped hillside, surrounded by corn fields running down to the river at the bottom of the valley.

The preparations for La Rejunta were well underway. Coloured decorations hung from windows and roofs, and people walked back and forth carrying sacks of cornmeal and great piles of wood. Elena found the last of her pesos and gave them to the taxi driver, but when he took them he crossed his chest and climbed back into the taxi, slamming the door shut.

Elena turned around. A black dog stood watching her on the other side of the street, teeth bared, drool sliding out of its jowls. Elena shooed it away.

At the house, she found her father sweeping outside. "Papa!"

Papa dropped his brush on the floor and held his arms out for her. He smelled of smoke and tobacco; he smelled like home. "What are you doing here?" he said.

"I'm here for La Rejunta. I got a ticket in the post. Didn't you know?"

"Didn't I know? I thought I was seeing a ghost!" He put his hand on her shoulders and then kissed her forehead. "You will have to tell me all about England, but first you should see your mother. She will want to know you're here."

"Oh. Of course. Where is she?"

"At the church, most likely. She is a major-domo this year."

The church sat at the top of the village, surrounded by a graveyard. Its position, high on the sloping valley, made it the best vantage point in the town, but it had been the source of many grumblings on Sunday mornings, when the younger Elena was forced to walk all the way up in her best clothes. *You should be thankful you don't have to carry a wooden cross like our Lord*, Mama used to say.

Elena trudged up the hill, trying to decide how to greet Mama. The last time they had spoken was several months before, and they hadn't parted on the best of terms. She found Mama at the church, surrounded by volunteers. She had a pocket watch on a chain, slung around her neck, and a clipboard and pen in her hands. When the volunteers received their instructions, they dispersed, leaving only space between the two of them.

"Elena?"

"Mama."

"I didn't know you would be here."

"Neither did I."

Elena sat down on a bench, trying to decide what to say.

"I can't believe you're here, Hija," Mama said. "How is England?"

Several years before, when Elena proudly announced that she would be going to UNAM to study Biology, the response from her parents was mixed. Papa embraced her, kissing her on the forehead before picking up the telephone so he could brag to his friends. Mama, however, was less enthusiastic. Why did Elena need to go and study? What was she lacking in her life at home?

When Elena graduated with first class honours and was offered a doctoral placement in England, Mama's reaction had been even worse. It was one thing for her daughter to live seventeen miles away in the capital, but it was quite another for her to live all the way across the ocean. *Don't you know how cold it is in England?* she had said. *Don't you know what the food is like there? Boiled vegetables, boiled potatoes, boiled meat...* When her persistent attempts to dissuade Elena failed, her reluctance turned to anger, and then a cold disappointment. Elena, after all, was abandoning her family. Mama didn't even see her off at the airport.

Now, though, Mama was asking Elena about life in England, and it seemed like she was genuinely interested, as though she was asking questions for more than just the sake of politeness. If there was any awkwardness between them, Mama didn't appear to be aware of it.

Elena told her about the food, and the weather, and the university. After she had tried to explain how yes, she had been to Buckingham Palace, but no, she had not seen the Queen, Mama asked why she had returned. "Your Papa didn't tell you to come, did he?"

"No, he didn't say anything. I got a ticket in the post, and I just assumed it was from the two of you."

Mama looked confused. "But we wouldn't do such a thing – I mean, it's not that we wouldn't want you to come, of course. But you know how much those tickets cost."

For a moment, they sat in silence, and then their eyes met. "I think I might know who sent the ticket," Elena said.

#

Elena's Abuela lived just outside of the village. Her house was made from panels of wood, dotted with leaves and covered with grasping tendrils, as though Mother Nature had decided to reclaim the place for herself. When Elena knocked on the front door, Juana answered. Juana had been a part of the family since before Elena was born, even though she wasn't related by blood. She gave Elena a hug. "She's waiting for you in the garden."

The grass at the back had been recently cut, and the perimeter was packed with an array of plants, competing for the sun. There were two chairs out on the grass, but they were empty. Elena walked around the garden, studying the different plants and flowers, marvelling at how different the flora was compared with Oxford. She was interrupted by the sound of scratching, and she turned 'round just as a great dark-furred cat, like a jaguarondi or an ocelot, leapt down from roof of the house. Elena flinched instinctively, but then she smiled, recognising the markings on the beast's fur. It landed gracefully, cushioned on the ground, and then in one fluid movement it moved through the air and changed, like water being poured from a spout, until Elena's Abuela stood in front of her. "It's good to see you, Nieta," she said, and then she sat down in one of the chairs. "Come, join me."

Elena did as she was told. "You look well," she said.

"I do, do I? I'll take your word for it. The doctor says it's good for people of my age to get out and about and stretch their legs." She raised her eyes towards the roof. "So I'm just doing as I'm told."

Juana emerged from the house, bringing two glasses of iced water. She passed them round, then returned inside.

Elena sipped the water. "Thank you for my ticket, by the way."

"I have no idea what you're referring to," Abuela replied, barely concealing her smile. "Are you glad to be here?"

"Yes, of course. It's a bit strange after being away, but I've missed it."

"Yes, I thought you might. This is your home, after all. Did you know your mother was going to be a majordomo this year?"

"No, I had no idea. Is that why you wanted me to come?"

"Not exactly. Despite appearances, I'm not as spritely as I used to be, and I need someone to accompany me to the shrine tomorrow."

"Oh. So that's why you brought me here?"

"Yes. I needed some help, and I thought, who better than my favourite granddaughter?"

Elena smiled. "Your only granddaughter, you mean."

After they had made arrangements for the next day, Abuela retired inside for a nap. Elena began the journey home on foot, but as she rounded the corner from the house she bumped into Josefina, her aunt.

When she saw Elena she opened her mouth, baring her teeth in what Elena could only guess was supposed to be a smile. "Elena," she said. "What are you doing here?"

"I've come for La Rejunta."

"Oh. Of course. And then I suppose you'll be flying back?"

Elena wasn't sure what to say. "Well, I might stick around for a few days, but I can't stay for too long."

"How *is* England, anyway?"

"It's good. Very different to here, of course."

"And you're a scientist now, are you?"

"Well, sort of. I'm working towards a PhD in epigenetics, on part of a research team working on-"

Josefina cut her off. "I'm sorry, but I really must go." She paused for a few seconds, looking Elena up and down. "Enjoy your stay, Elena."

#

In the morning Papa made breakfast, and then Elena was put to work. She joined a huddle of women a few doors down, making tamales for the shared table. It took a while for her to remember the different steps of the process, but after a couple of goes the old patterns returned to her; how to balance a corn husk in one hand and scoop just the right amount of masa with her other; how to balance the ratio of meat and salsa, without overloading the filling; how to wrap the tamale up tightly, tying it with a strip from another husk. Soon she settled into a steady rhythm, constructing the tamales and listening to the other women gossiping. Every now and again she saw Mama pass by outside, directing traffic and volunteers.

When she had a tray full of tamales in front of her, one of the other women checked her work. She nodded in approval, and Elena felt a surprising surge of pride. She stepped out into the street for a break, and found Juana waiting for her.

"It's time, Elena," she said.

Juana led her to a four-by-four, where Abuela waited in the back seat. She wore an old, weathered necklace, one that Elena had seen many times before. It was the family's oldest heirloom.

Elena climbed into the back of the vehicle. "I thought you needed help getting there?" she said.

"No, Juana will drive us to the caves."

"So what am I here for?"

"You're here to keep me company."

The journey to the caves took a couple of hours, winding through tight, ramshackle dirt tracks. Juana drove with complete abandon, hurtling round corners and spewing up mud with the tyres. Elena gripped the inside of the door, and for a while she thought she might bring her breakfast back up.

By the time they arrived, there was already a crowd of people waiting outside the caves. There were old women thumbing rosaries, men selling crosses on chains, and young children there for the first time, wondering what was going on.

Juana stayed with the vehicle while Elena and Abuela got out. The crowds moved away from the entrance to the cave, but the rocky outcrops on the external walls were being used as perches by four or five dozen birds. Abuela walked ahead and whispered something to them, and in one swift movement, as though each bird was just one part of a great feathered cloud, they flew up into the air, and away.

It was dark inside the cave, but just enough natural light leaked in through the entrance, and through unknown cracks and crevices above, so that Elena could see where she was going. In the deepest part of the cave, the walls were illuminated by flickering candles surrounding the shrine, with a statue and a weathered crucifix.

Abuela blew out the candles, until only one remained. "You remember the story of these caves, Elena?"

"Yes. This was a place of communion for our family, going back thousands of years. The gods of the rivers and the skies and the cornfields were worshipped here, and our leaders consulted with the spirits."

"And then what happened?"

"There was a miracle. A statue of Christ appeared."

"El Señor de Chalma, yes. Indeed, this whole region is a place of miracles. At the last festival, one of the women in town spilled boiling mole all over herself, but when the medics arrived, she was unharmed. The year before that, there was a crop failure coupled with a record numbers of pilgrims, but all were fed from only a fraction of the food that was needed. But you know, Elena, miracles happened here well before priests appeared in their robes." When she was finished speaking, she stepped away, into the darkness.

Elena watched Abuela's shadow on the wall of the cave. At first the only movement was from the flickering of the candle, but then the shadow itself began to change, taking new forms: snouts and hooves, claws and tails, beaks and wings. The cave filled with whispers, hushed at first but then louder and more frantic, joining into a pulsing rhythm, louder and louder. Then the candle was extinguished, and there was darkness, and there was silence.

Elena didn't know how long the darkness lasted for. The voices were no longer audible but she could hear them still, thrumming at the back of her head. She didn't understand the words, but each syllable had its own texture, a fabric matching the stone walls of the cave, the air outside, and the sun beating down from the sky.

In the darkness, the candle flickered into life once more. Abuela stood before her, sweat on her brow. "When was the last time you used your gift, Elena?"

Elena didn't know what to say.

"Elena? The ancestors demand an answer."

Elena looked away. As a child, she had enjoyed testing the limits of her abilities. She would swing through the trees with a pack of spider monkeys, or glide over the corn fields on her wings. But as she grew older she became less and less comfortable, and at UNAM and then in Oxford the world of her youth had begun to seem strange, almost unreal. "I don't know," she said. "Not for a while."

"It is a gift, Elena. But gifts can be rescinded if they are not taken. Why don't you use it?

"I don't know."

The candle flame continued to flicker. "I know how gifted you are, Elena. You are gifted in many different ways, and you are capable of many different things. This research you are doing on the other side of the world – well, it is beyond my own capabilities, or those of the rest of our family. There are not many people I know who could achieve what you have achieved. It is truly impressive. But there are fewer people still who share your other gifts, the ones you were born with."

"Why are you saying all this?"

"Because I may not have long left on this earth, Elena."

Elena felt her stomach tense. "What do you mean? You shouldn't say things like that."

"Please, Elena, I'm not saying this to garner your sympathy. I have lived a good, long life, fuller than most people can say. But soon I will be taking flight for the last time. I will go to join the ancestors, and then someone else will have to take my place." She took hold of Elena's hand. "As you know, in normal circumstances my eldest daughter would follow on from me."

"Mama."

"Yes. That is the way things have been done for as long as we know. But your mother does not have the gift, Elena. Many times when she was younger I believed she was hiding it, or that she was too scared to use it. But after many years, I came to realise the truth. Only the gods know why, but she simply does not have it. She has grown up to be a good woman, an admirable woman. You know this. But I fear it is not enough. I fear *she* is not enough."

"What about my aunt? She has the gift."

Abuela rolled her eyes. "Elena, one of the benefits of growing old is that people begin to expect less of you in certain regards. They are more forgiving of blunt words, for example. So let me state this clearly, for the avoidance of doubt. Your aunt is not a good person. Were she not my daughter, I would have nothing to do with her. Alas, such is life that we are tied together by blood. I love Josefina, Elena, I really do. But I do not *like* her. She is mean, and self-absorbed, and there is a bitterness running through her heart. I fear what would happen if she were the one to continue the traditions. There are ancient things in this land, ancient powers, and they must be regarded with respect. Not long ago, most of the villages in this region had their own nahual, but now not only a few of us remain."

The things Abuela said about Josefina rang true. She had always sneered at Mama, looked down on her for marrying Papa, and she had always treated Elena with a measure of disdain. Still, there was something shocking about Abuela's bluntness. "So what are you going to do?"

"I want you to take my place, Elena. To carry on the traditions."

"I don't understand."

"What's to understand? Soon I will be gone, and someone must take my place. To commune with the ancestors, to speak with the animals, to watch over these lands. Why shouldn't that person be you?"

Just a few days ago, the idea of returning just for a visit seemed remote to Elena. But to stay forever?

She stood in silence for a few moments, trying to comprehend the idea. "But I don't even live here anymore," she said. "I have my work in England, and I'm really not sure I–"

Abuela lifted her finger to her lips. "Shhh, you do not have to make your decision at this very moment." She smiled, lifted the necklace from her neck, and gave it to Elena. "Do you know where I got this, Elena?"

Elena lifted the necklace up to the light. It was a strange thing, made up of pieces of stone, all odd shapes, strung together on a piece of twine. "You got it from your mother. My great-grandmother."

"Yes. And where did she get it from?"

"From *her* mother."

"Yes."

While Elena examined the necklace, Abuela continued to speak. "And she got it from *her* mother, who got it from *her* mother, and so on and so on all the way back until time is only mist and shadow. Before corporations and cars,

Elena. Before kings, and emperors, and struggles for independence. Before the first ships arrived on this shore, bringing plagues and war and death and a crucified messiah. Before the people of this land built great stone structures and made sacrifices to the old gods. Before then, even. We have always been here, Elena. We are the cougars, padding through the undergrowth, silently hunting prey. We are the hawks, surveying the land. We are nahuales."

#

By the time they arrived back home, the festivities were well underway. Music and singing hummed through the streets, and the air carried the scent of slow-cooked barbacoa, mingling with ritual incense.

A huge table ran down the centre of the main street, made up of smaller ones donated by the local residents. This long, irregular wooden structure was piled up with bowls and platters, and surrounded by pilgrims, laughing and eating.

Elena walked with Abuela and Juana, trying to find a seat. When people saw them they waved, or bowed, or offered their own place at the table.

"I never realised how much of a celebrity you are, Abuela."

"The head of our family always has a place of honour at La Rejunta."

"It's a bit strange though, isn't it, at a Catholic festival? I don't remember there being any nahuales in the Bible."

Abuela laughed. "Perhaps if God had decided to incarnate himself here in Mexico, he would have become a nahual instead of a carpenter. Maybe she would have fed the five thousand with tortillas, and crossed the lake underneath the surface of the water, clad in scales."

When they arrived near the top of the table, Josefina was waiting for them. She shot a fierce glare at Elena, before embracing Abuela. "I have a seat prepared for you, Mama. Come, sit with me."

Elena stepped aside, embarrassed, but Abuela grabbed hold of her. "Actually," she said, "I had hoped to dine with Elena."

For a moment, it looked like Josefina would stand her ground, blocking their way, but she decided to step aside.

They passed by. Elena heard Josefina hiss something, but she couldn't understand the words. "What did she say?" she asked Juana.

"Nothing you need to worry about."

The food at the feast was fragrant and delicious, and there was plenty of wine to go with it. One evening back in Oxford, when Elena had been suffering one of her bouts of homesickness, some friends from the department took her to a Mexican restaurant in Jericho. Most of the things on the menu were unrecognisable, and when the food arrived it was a strange experience, the culinary equivalent of reading a badly-translated Fuentes novel. Elena told her friends it was delicious, but it was nothing like this. This was the real thing.

Abuela took great pleasure in introducing her to the surrounding guests, causing Elena to blush. Josefina sat further down the table, and Elena tried to avoid looking at her. Mama passed by every now again, but their attempts to make her sit down and eat all ended in failure. "There is so much still do," she said.

Later on, when the guests had eaten enough, Abuela announced that she was going home, escorted by Juana. Elena walked home by herself, the skies beginning to darken, the air beginning to cool.

Back home, Elena put the necklace on. It was surprisingly heavy around her neck. She thought about Abuela's offer – or was it a demand? – and tried to imagine writing a message to her supervisor at the labs. How would she even go about explaining such a thing? *I'm abandoning our research so I can commune with my ancestors, so I can live among the animals and the birds. I hope you'll understand.* But the thought of saying no to Abuela was even more daunting. How could she turn her back on her birthright? To follow her wishes seemed too great a weight to carry, but then Elena closed her eyes and pictured Josefina wearing the necklace, Josefina communing with the ancestors, the animals, the spirits. Josefina deciding the future of the traditions. She shivered.

When Mama returned it was late, almost midnight. Elena went to meet her at the door, and Mama's gaze fell on the necklace around Elena's neck. "What is that, Elena? What are you wearing?"

Elena took hold of Mama's hands. "Abuela gave it to me."

"I didn't know."

Elena smiled. "I've decided not to return to England, Mama. I'm going to stay here with you and Papa. For good."

Elena waited for Mama to smile back, but instead her lips began to tremble. She pulled her hands away from Elena's.

"What's wrong?"

Mama paced up and down the room, shaking her head. "No," she repeated, "No. You cannot do this Elena. I won't let this happen."

"Please, Mama, I've already--"

"No! This is not right."

Elena couldn't understand what had happened. For all those years, Mama had tried to discourage her from leaving; now she had returned for good, and Mama couldn't bear it.

"Mama, please, I—"

Someone knocked on the front door, urgently tapping at the wood.

Elena went to open it, her head spinning. She found Juana standing there, crying.

"What is it Juana? What's wrong?"

Juana wiped her face with her hand. "She's dead, Elena."

#

The doctor said it was a heart attack. Juana had helped Abuela into bed that night, and gone to make a drink; when she returned, Abuela was no longer breathing.

The funeral was held only a couple of days later. In the meantime Mama was busier than ever, continuing to perform her majordomo duties while preparing for the funeral. Elena tried to find opportunities to speak to her, to talk about what had happened, but Mama hid behind the shroud of her busyness.

It was a simple ceremony, with a short mass. The room was covered in flowers, brought as gifts by the villagers. Elena stood next to Mama, desperately searching for the right words, and floundering.

Afterwards, they returned to Abuela's home. Papa and Mama shared condolences with friends of the family, while Juana moved back and forth through the house, bringing drinks to the guests and taking more flowers and tokens of grief. Elena barely knew the rest of the people there, and she wasn't in the mood for making small talk, not while Abuela's loss sat like a sinkhole in the middle of her chest, sucking everything in until all that was left was a numb darkness. With the stale air in the house clogging her nostrils, Elena stepped out into the garden.

It was early evening, the sun low in the sky. Elena looked up at the roof, where Abuela had been just a few days ago. She had said she might pass away soon, but Elena hadn't even considered that it might happen so quickly. Had

Abuela known that her last breath was so imminent? Was that why she brought Elena here with so little warning?

"Where is it, you little bitch?"

Elena turned to see Josefina behind her. "I'm sorry?"

"Don't play the fool. Where is it? I know you have it."

"Have what?"

"The necklace."

"I don't know—"

"Liar!" Josefina moved forwards, eyes full of rage, forcing Elena to step back.

"Please, I haven't done anything wrong."

Josefina thrust her finger towards Elena. "Everyone else might fall for your sweet little act, but I know what you're up to. You came here, wheedled your way into her favour, and then waited for her to die so you could take what's rightfully mine. You're a scheming, cowardly little bitch."

"That's not true. She invited me. And how would I be stealing from you, anyway? You're not even the eldest."

"So what? Your dumb mother may be the eldest, but that's not enough. Nowhere near enough. She has no gift. She is not a nahual. But I am." Josefina held her hand out again but now it was darker, with five jagged claws. "So are you going to give me what's mine, or do I need to take it from you?"

"Please, I-"

Josephina lurched forwards, swiping at the air with her claws. Elena stepped backwards but she lost her footing, falling to the ground.

Josephina stood over her. "Look at you. You're pathetic. You think you're a nahual, but you can't even stand up against me, can't even use your gifts when you need them most."

Elena looked past Josephina, at the sky. She thought about changing, surging into the sky on wings, but when she tried to grasp the gift inside her she could only fumble at it.

Josephina opened her mouth. A bead of spit dribbled out of the edge of her mouth. "Where's the necklace, Elena?"

"I don't-"

"Tell me where it is!"

"What's going on here?"

Elena recognised Mama's voice, and felt a surge of relief.

Josephina didn't even turn her head. "It's nothing of your concern."

Mama balled her hand into a fist. "You come here, on today of all days, and act like this? Shame on you, Josefina." She shook her head, and turned to Elena, helping her up. "Are you okay?"

"Yes, thank you."

"You think you scare me?" Josefina said.

Mama span round and took a stride toward her sister, so their faces were inches apart. Her voice was controlled, but there was something fierce, something primal beneath. "No. But you should leave now, if you ever want to be allowed back here."

"You think that's your decision?"

"It is," Mama replied. "And Josefina, don't you dare touch my daughter again."

Josefina grimaced, and mouthed something towards Elena. She spat on the floor, and walked away.

"Thank you, Mama," Elena said.

Mama stared back in silence.

"Mama?"

"I can't do this, Elena." She turned and walked away.

Elena wanted to go after her, but her feet were rooted to the ground. She watched her go.

Elena sat down in one of the garden chairs, the same one she had been in just the other day, when the world was different.

When she was ready, Elena went back inside to find Mama, to try to speak to her again. But she was already gone. Papa said she had left the gathering early to rejoin her duties as a major-domo, not even a bereavement being enough to deter her from her commitments.

Elena left the house. She didn't want to go home, but she didn't know where else to go. So, she walked.

Most of the locals and visitors had retired to their beds, but there were still little pockets of celebration, groups of men and woman sharing leftover bottles of wine, or singing songs while someone plucked at a guitar.

Elena passed by two men standing at a street corner, laughing, and for a moment she thought about going over to them and demanding to know how they had the nerve to act so brazenly at a time like this. Abuela was dead, Mama was furious, and Elena was a stranger in her own home. How could anyone be laughing?

For the next few hours, Elena walked around the village in circles and knots, passing by the dwindling remnants of the day's festivities, walking and walking until her feet were swollen and dry.

Eventually, she arrived back home. Papa sat waiting for her on the wall outside. "Where have you been?" he said. "I was worried about you."

"I went for a walk. I needed to get some fresh air."

"Fresh air? It's after midnight."

Elena didn't respond.

"Are you okay? You look upset."

Elena sat down next to him. Her feet throbbed. "It's all gone wrong Papa."

Papa put his arms around her. "Tell me what happened, Hija."

Elena wiped her eyes. "I finally decided I would stay, to do what Abuela asked of me. But when I told Mama, it was like I had slapped her in the face. It's like she thinks I betrayed her, like she can't bear being near me."

Papa began to laugh.

"Why are you laughing? This isn't funny."

"Hold on for a moment. There's something you should see." Papa went rummaging in the other room, and came back with a book. He handed it to Elena. "Look."

There was a newspaper clipping stuck onto the first page. "Hold on, isn't this-"

"Yes. You sent it to us, remember?"

It was a clipping of a story from the university newspaper, about Elena's research project. The rest of the book was full of clippings and photos, some from newspapers, the others printed off the internet. "You collected all this?"

"Me? No, I had little to do with it. It was your Mama's work."

"I don't understand."

"Elena, listen to me. She isn't upset because you're staying here, or because you're taking your Abuela's place. She's upset because you being here means you're leaving England, leaving your place there."

"But she never even wanted me to go there in the first place."

"No, she didn't. She didn't want you to be so far away, and she didn't understand why you wanted to go, why you felt such a need to find your own way."

"So what's changed?"

"I think it was that first newspaper clipping that started it. Neither of us really understood what your research was all about – we still don't, to be honest – but we knew it was something that would help people. We saw your name there, and your picture, and honestly, I've never seen your Mama look so proud. And you know what she said to me? She said she was wrong to try to stop you going in the first place, that she could see that now. She's proud of you, Elena."

Elena covered her mouth with her hand. "But I had no idea. Why didn't she say anything?"

"A few months ago, when we found out she would be a majordomo for this year's festival, I wanted to tell you about it, and I started saving for a ticket to bring you home. But your Mama wouldn't allow it. She wanted to see you, but she couldn't bear the idea of interrupting your work."

"But I had no idea." Elena flicked the pages of the book back and forth. "What do I do now?"

"That, Hija, is up to you."

To her own surprise, Elena knew precisely what to do. She found Mama in the front room, stretched out in her armchair, still wearing her funeral clothes. Her eyes were closed. "Mama?" Elena said, but there was no response. The months of preparation, the pressures of being a majordomo, and now the weight of grief had finally caught up with her. She was fast asleep, her body trying to recover from its exhaustion.

Elena knelt down in front of her. With tears in her eyes, she lifted the necklace and looped it over Mama's head.

"I think they're wrong, Mama," she said. "I think you are enough."

#

Elena was used to brittle layers of frost in the morning, and she had seen light snowfall a few times before, the kind that danced on the breeze and settled into thin patterns before melting away, but this – this was something different. The whole of Oxford was engulfed in white, as though a great volcano had erupted, spewing geysers of purified, bleached ash.

With her thickest coat on, Elena set out for Port Meadow. She passed by a few hardy souls on her way, tough locals out walking their dogs, but for most of the journey Elena was alone, crunching the snow under her feet and watching the falling flakes glide and swirl through the air.

Somewhere out on the edge of the meadow there was a pair of robins, singing. Elena listened to them, enchanted by the tune, and then she watched them fly across the sky.

Elena turned in a full circle, making sure no one was watching – not that anyone would believe what they were seeing anyway – and then she closed her eyes. She thought of the sky, of the feeling of the breeze, and as she stepped forwards she felt her body changing. Something swelled within her, like her cells were igniting.

Then her body was like water, like smoke, like light breaking through the branches of a tree. She pushed off with her wings, and surged up, into the sky.

END

Freeman's Truth
by David Rheinhart

Momma, bless her heart, never did understand my infatuation with Booker Freeman. Truth be told, at the time, I didn't either. There was something magnetic about that wrinkled black man. Something honest in his calloused hands. Honesty is such a hard thing to come by these days that sometimes we don't recognize it for what it is.

Music takes honesty, and there was no better a musician than Booker Freeman.

He used to play an old flattop outside the Liberty Store, trading songs for swigs of sour

wine. Few made the trade, and even fewer listened, but still he was there month after month,
year after year, filling the street with the metallic
twang of his guitar.

It were Momma that introduced us, accidentally of course. She sent me down to the Liberty Store to get a gallon of whole milk for her
cooking. Now, I wasn't about to let this oppor-
tunity for mischief pass me by, so I gathered my
friend Jacob and explained my plan.

"We're on a quest," I said, puffing out my
chest. "We're knights, and as knights we have a
duty to fetch ourselves a holy object."

Jacob frowned. "That don't sound like no
knights I ever heard of. Knights don't fetch, they
fight. Are you sure you know what you're on
about?"

"What about the grail?"

"Now I know you is making stuff up."

"You mean to tell me you ain't never heard of
no grail?"

He was getting upset now. "If you know something, then come out and say it. There's no sense in pretending you're smarter than me."

"You remember the Bible story with the loaves and fishes?"

"Course."

"Then you know that Jesus can magic up fishes, as many fishes as he wants." Jacob started to speak, but I silenced him with a look. "Now then, at the Last Supper, Jesus summoned the biggest and tastiest fish that ever swam-- I'm talking a real whopper-- but the Romans got him before he could eat it. Since they knew Jesus could come back, the Romans took the fish and hid it somewhere far, far away. That was the grail."

"Makes sense so far," Jacob said.

"Later, King Arthur and his knights pledged to find and return the fish to Jesus, so they scoured the land."

"They ever find it?"

To be honest, the skymercial shutdown before I could get to that part, but it wouldn't do to let Jacob know that. "Sure they did! You don't think King Arthur couldn't find a fish if he wanted to, do you?"

"No, I s'pose he could find it. What happened to the fish?"

"They hid it."

"Why would they go and do a silly thing like that?"

"So more knights could fetch it. Knights are all about fetching stuff, and the best ones go and fetch the Grail."

We arrived at the Liberty Store. Old Booker Freeman sat outside. On his leg perched a guitar covered in stickers and tape. He slapped its strings with a great, dark hand, and then muttered a few words into his knee. His voice was guttural and rough, but it had sweetness to it, like candy.

"So what's our holy object?" Jacob asked.

"I'm working on that," I said, my gaze falling and locking on Mr. Freeman. His thick fingers moved with a dexterity that seemed alien for their size. They drew me in. Without really meaning to, I found myself sitting on the dirt listening to him play. His song seemed to take an eternity. I couldn't understand a lick of what he was saying, but the way he said it made me feel funny; like I'd lost something and couldn't get it back. Only Heaven knows what I'd lost, though.

Finally, Mr. Freeman strummed the last chord and looked at us with yellowed eyes. "You boys need something?" I shifted uncomfortably. Now that I was talking to him, I had just realized I had nothing to talk about.

"D'ya know where we can find a grail?" Jacob blurted out. I shushed him, but it did little good.

"That one of them fancy cup things?" Mr. Freeman asked.

"Nah, it's a fish," I said. "One of the big, floppy types." I extended my arms out to show how long it probably was.

"Only fish I know of swim down at the pond; they're plenty floppy. Not too big, though." Mr. Freeman took a long swig from the bottle at his side. When it was empty, he frowned and threw it at an open trash cans. It struck the ground with a crash. "Used to be a man could make a living picking up those kinds of things. Not a good one, but a living."

Jacob and I grinned at each other. Adults didn't typically talk of the time before the camp, and to hear one speak so candidly was a treat.

"How'd you make a living off bottles?" I prompted him.

"What's a living?" Jacob added.

Mr. Freeman smiled. It was a big, yellow smile, one that stretched from cheek to cheek. "When I was your age, I'd go 'round the neighborhood and collect old cans and bottles. There was a shack in back of the Safeway. A man there--he was rarely the same fella twice--would give me twenty-five cents a pound for glass and thirty cents for aluminum."

"He paid you for garbage?"

"It ain't garbage if you know what to do with it. The man in the shack would take the stuff to a bigger shack where they'd melt it all down. Then, they'd make stuff with it."

"Like what?" I asked.

He shrugged. "I don't know. Baseball bats and shit? All I knew was that I got paid. It was good, honest work." Mr. Freeman absentmindedly groped at his side, searching for the bottle he'd thrown. When he realized it was gone, he sighed and picked up his guitar. "Can't do that now, though. Can't do anything now."

Almost on cue, a helper bot rolled from its hole and drove towards the bottle. It scooped up the glass and dumped the shards in the trash.

When everything was clean, it circled the can twice and returned to its hiding place. When I looked close, I could just make out the faint, red glow of its sensor.

"You boys get along now," Mr. Freeman said, frowning at the robot. "I've got all these fine people waiting for me to play; one of them's bound to buy a poor man a drink."

A gust of wind blew a small dust devil across the beaten dirt path. "Ain't nobody here, mister," Jacob said.

Mr. Freeman hummed tunelessly.

#

Jacob and I only played in the pond for a little while—there weren't no fish big enough to be the Grail—before I went and grabbed the milk. The plastic handle dug into my hand something awful. Painting Cow Whole Milk, the only milk genetically guaranteed to turn your tongue white. It turned other things white, too. Jacob and I tested it on a slug he found crawling outside his shelter once. When we poured the milk over the slug it made an odd sizzling sound. Didn't move too much after that.

To me, the camp where we lived was never temporary. It'd always existed, and it'd never given me cause to doubt it would continue to do so. When you're young and don't know better, everything, especially the transitory, is permanent. Someone smarter than me evidently disagreed, for although we'd been there near as long as I could remember, plastic FEMA shelters were all they'd given us. They were beginning to show their age, too. Nearly all of the off-white plastic buildings were corroded, yellowed and cracked by countless days in the sun.

It's not that I minded the houses too much—they're all I really knew—but living out of what amounted to a cheap igloo can wear on even the most ignorant of souls. Spending time out of the house and away from Momma was always a blessing.

That's why I hesitated for a spell before opening the door and calling for her. It was kinda something I had to work up to.

"Get the milk?" she said, tracking me as I set it on the table. "Boy, what have I told you about playing in the mud?"

I looked down. I hadn't noticed it before, but my pants were coated in a thick layer of grime from the pond. "I'm sorry, Momma. I was with Jacob. We was looking for the Grail."

"You best get out of those clothes before I turn your behind red." Momma emptied the gallon of milk into the great pot she had cooking on the stove as I changed. The igloo filled with a pleasant aroma. "How you gonna find a Grail in the mud? Honestly. And I don't like you hanging around that Jacob boy. He's a bad influence. Did you know his mother had him outta wedlock?"

"Yes, Momma," I said more to fill the lull than because I agreed. My participation in this part of the conversation wasn't really necessary.

"Now his dad's gone and some fella took his place. Seems there's a new man over there every week." She tossed a handful of chopped vegetables and seasonings into the soup. "The pastor really ought to do something about that family."

I sat at the table while Momma prattled on. She put a bowl in front of me and filled it with the white broth. I poked at it with my spoon. "Hey Momma, what's a living?" I said eventually.

"Where'd you hear a funny word like that?"

"From Mr. Freeman at the grocery store. He said he used to make a living off cans."

"Booker Freeman is a no good degenerate that wouldn't know a living unless it came in a bottle. Bless his heart. Don't talk to that man. He's full of odd notions."

"But what's a living?"

"A living is what we make every night—what you'll make tonight—and it's what Booker Freeman is too proud to do."

"You mean the skymercials?"

"That's right. If Mr. Freeman wants to go collecting garbage like some sort of robot, then let him. But I don't want you anywhere near that man. You're a proper, god-fearing boy." She pulled me close. The sun dipped below the horizon as the sky turned orange. "It's almost time. Go fetch your things."

I dropped the spoon into my empty bowl with a clatter. "Yes, Momma," I said.

#

Dusk was always my favorite part of the day. The neighborhood sprang to life just after dinner. Neighbors gathered on the dirt road outside their prefab houses and gossiped. I didn't much care for the gossip, but I never felt more like I lived in a community than in that hour just before nightfall. The others times of the day were lonely in comparison.

Jacob stood bored next to his mother. When he spied me, his face stretched into a smile. He waved, so I crossed over to him.

"My mom got real mad at me for talking to Mr. Freeman," Jacob said.

"Yeah, mine too," I said. "Why do you think they hate him so?"

"Probably the drink. Mom says I shouldn't trust a man with shaking hands." A pair of little kids ran by chasing a small, metal dog. The dog's wheels kicked up a spray of dirt and dust. It'd been a long time since the last rain.

"Didn't your dad have a thing for the bottle?" I asked.

Jacob got real quiet. "He liked a lot of things," he said eventually. "The bottle was one of them."

I nodded sagely. "My Momma says Mr. Freeman has no idea how to make a living. She says he thinks he's too good to watch the skymercials." I kicked a rock into a gopher hole. "But that don't sit right. Mr. Freeman didn't strike me as the type to be too good for anything."

"So what you want to do?"

I thought for a moment. "Well, the way I see it, we should ask him. King Arthur never sentenced anybody without at least hearing their side first, and I don't see why we should be the exception."

"But my mom said I'm not to go near him."

"That's why we ought to do it on the down low," I said. "Tomorrow at dawn, we'll hold a trial for Mr. Freeman and get to the bottom of the matter."

The crowd drifted one by one to the large cushioned chairs lined up in front of every home. "Jacob, sweetie!" Jacob's mom called.

"It's starting," he said. "Tomorrow."

"Tomorrow."

Jacob ran off. I set up my chair and laid back, staring at the sky. As the light faded, I could make out the first, faint moving pictures. The speakers on either side of my head picked up the sound, changing as I shifted about. I found a familiar voice--it advertised some kind of laxative--and focused. A green number ticked on a small display inlaid into my armrest, counting the pennies earned.

I'm not proud to say I slept through the dawn. I slept through the morning, too, but it's the dawn part that kills me. When I did eventually roll out of bed, the sun had crossed the halfway point in the sky and begun its long trek down the other side. Momma was still sleeping, though. The front door shut with a soft click behind me.

Jacob's window was covered in a thick sheet. I knocked lightly against the pane and half-whispered, half-shouted his name. His brother flicked the cloth aside. He frowned at me in his boxers, but kicked Jacob awake anyway. Jacob rose from his bed rubbing his eyes, pulled on some clothes, and stumbled out the door.

"How long you been up?" he asked me.

"Since dawn," I said. "Been waiting for you." He apologized and the two of walked to the Liberty store.

But Mr. Freeman wasn't in his usual spot on the bench out front. There was, however, the scattered metal pieces of a broken helper bot. Someone had taken a rock to the poor thing's shell and tore it open like a crawdad. Whomever it was had pinned the thing between the bench and a trash can and relieved themselves inside of it. The smell was pungent.

"Over here!" Jacob called from around the corner.

Mr. Freeman lay against the side of the building under a pile of dirty blankets. Flattened boxes made his bed, and around him were the scattered carcasses of helper bots stuffed with shards of green glass. Jacob poked the old man with a stick.

"Is he dead?" I asked.

Mr. Freeman groaned. "Don't seem like it," Jacob said. "But that could just be gas escaping."

"Farts don't swat at sticks. We've gotta get him up; a sleeping man can't go on trial."

Jacob poked harder. Mr. Freeman rolled over, burying his head beneath a sweat-yellowed pillow. "I don't think he's gonna wake anytime soon."

"There has to be some way." I looked around. One of the helper bot shells still had a green bottle that was mostly intact. I pulled the bottle from its sheath. On the glass' side was a paper logo with big, flower letters and the faint outline of some castle on a miserable looking island. "Maybe he needs incentive."

"You're putting on airs again."

"Man, it ain't my fault you're ignorant." Seeing the frown on his face, I started again. "You know when it's cold and you don't wanna get outta bed, but your momma's cooking bacon and you can smell it from the kitchen? That's incentive." I hefted the bottle. "We don't got no bacon, but I know something that might work just as well."

#

Liberty Inc. handled the supply of most mountainous refugee camps—like ours—and since there was literally nothing to compete against up here, they wasted little effort in decorating or maintaining their store. The result was a featureless, grey warehouse manned by an army of barely cognizant sales associates. Not that I was aware of this at the time. To me, they were always just The Bots, and I dealt with them like anybody handling poorly engineered technology: restrained frustration.

One of those associates skidded to stop before us as we walked through the automated wooshy doors. "Welcome to the Liberty Discount Superstore! The Only Store That Gives YOU The Freedom To Save!™" Small tendrils of smoke rose from the car battery screwed into its side. The air smelled faintly of ozone. "My name's Paul, and I'll be your Bargain Guidance Counselor! How might I assist you?"

Each gesture of its hyper expressive arms spewed little puffs of rust. "We're looking for one of these," I said, holding up the bottle. "Do you know where we can—"

"I'm sorry," the robot said, "I didn't quite catch that."

"Do you know—"

"I'm sorry. I didn't quite catch that."

I frowned at the clanking automaton. "I don't think this thing is going to be of much use," I said to Jacob. "You got any ideas?"

"Let me try," Jacob said. I handed him the bottle. Jacob kicked the robot in its side, sending a hollow bang through its shell.

The robot turned to Jacob. "We here at Liberty Discount Superstore understand your frustration. We apologize for the inconvenience." The robot made a loud and horrible screeching sound. From its chest spat a yellow piece of paper. "Please accept this coupon as a thank you for choosing to shop Liberty Discount Superstore." The hardwon fragment floated unaccepted to the ground.

Jacob stood on the tips of his toes, holding the green bottle before the associate's eye. The robot beeped. "My sensors indicate that you are looking for Chateau D'lf Bottom Shelf Cooking Sherry. Is this correct?"

"Yes," Jacob said.

"I'm sorry. I didn't quite catch that."

"Yes!"

"Fantastic! Are there any other items that I might help you with today?"

"No."

"Would you like to join our Super Discount Patriot Loyalty Program to take advantage of a point oh five percent savings on your next purchase?"

"No."

"Would you like to enter to win a limited edition matchbook by filling out a quick, forty-five minute survey rating your Liberty Discount Superstore buying experience?"

"No."

"Excellent! Please wait here while my assistants gather your products." The robot snapped to attention. Its arm creaked, then fell to the concrete with a loud clang. It didn't seem to notice.

A small basket with wheels whirled around a corner and pulled to a stop before us. The assistant beeped as it charged my account. We collected our bottle and turned to go. "Thank you for choosing Liberty Discount Super Store! The Only Store That—" The door shut behind us with a breezy whoosh.

#

The old man had started to snore. Frankly, the camp echoed with it. I unscrewed the cooking sherry's top and held it under Mr. Freeman's nose. He stirred and sat up, wiping the grime from his eyes. "Whatchu want?" he said groggily. He eyed the bottle, opening and closing his mouth with an audible sticky sound. "Boys your age shouldn't have something like that. Let me keep it safe." I handed him the bottle, and he upended it down his throat.

When it was empty, I drew myself to the fullest my three-foot five frame would allow. "Mr. Freeman, you stand accused of thinking you're better than other people," I roared with a voice like squeaky thunder. "How do you plead?"

The old man rubbed at a scar on the tip of his nose. "Thirsty."

"You're either innocent or guilty. I don't know no court of law that accepts 'thirsty' as a declaration."

"They should," Mr. Freeman said more to himself than to us. "It'd make life quite a bit easier." A helper bot beeped around the corner and nosed into the pile of trash at Mr. Freeman's feet. The old man chucked his empty bottle and struck the poor robot square in its glass eye. "Got'em."

"Mr. Freeman, are you innocent or are you guilty?"

Finally, the old man looked at us. "You boys are considerably more annoying than you was yesterday." He patted his pockets, pulling out a lighter and crumpled box of smokes. "What's got you all riled up?"

"It's the Skymercials, sir," Jacob said. "Our moms say you won't watch, and we was wondering on account of why?"

"They're disgusting." He lit his cigarette and took a long puff. "Some suit went and covered up something beautiful, and now I gotta stomach it every time I look up."

"There's something behind all them skymercials?" I said. "I thought it just kind of... ended." Jacob nodded. He looked to have had the same theory.

"Not something, nothing."

"So we was right?" Jacob asked.

"I mean, not entirely nothing. There's stuff in the nothing; not much, but there's some." Mr. Freeman groped for words. "And sometimes it's nice to look at nothing. Ain't nobody telling you what to do, where to sit, or who to talk to. It's just... nothing."

"Let me get this straight," I said. "You won't watch the skymercials because you want to look at nothing?"

"No, there's something in the nothing, and I want to look at the something, but I also want to see the nothing." Mr. Freeman looked pained. "This isn't coming out right. Look, there's these things called 'stars'."

"What's a star?" Jacob asked.

Mr. Freeman looked up. "Lord Jesus, I am not drunk enough for this." He threw the still burning cigarette at the helper bot carcass and took a deep breath. "Don't worry about it. All you need to know is that stars are pretty and looking at the skymercials makes me sad."

"I don't get it," I said. "But it don't sound like you're guilty. Jacob?"

"Nope, not guilty. You think that's where King Arthur hid the Grail?"

I frowned at the sky, trying to peer through its vast, blue expanse. "Maybe. I can't think of no reason why else they would cover it up."

The old man sighed and stood, stretching the kinks out of his joints with a loud series of pops. "I've got a busy morning and you two are bothering me. Scram."

We left, arguing with each other about how someone might hide a fish in the sky.

#

A tampon skymercial took up most the real estate that evening, some three quarters of it. For the life of me, I couldn't much tell why the pubescent bear was so happy not to leak fluid, but then, I suppose, if I were to suddenly start gushing blue water then I'd want something to stem it right quick too, pads or otherwise.

But the backflipping animal wasn't the target of my attention. Not really. That honor belongs to whatever lay behind it. Try as I might, I couldn't quite see through the picture. Each time I came close some singing animal in a sombrero would roll across the screen, snagging my attention like a tumble weed snags dirt.

I never stopped thinking about it, though. Even as the sun was climbing over the horizon, Mr. Freeman's words kept bouncing in my skull. The last image I remember before falling into a fitful—and ultimately unsatisfying—sleep, was the blinking, red light on top of the mountain just visible from my bedroom window.

#

The next night wasn't any better, nor the night after that, and by the end of the week I was ready to jump off something tall to make the thinking stop. I didn't, though; the preacher says suicide is a sin. Instead, I went to Momma.

She was in her usual place at the stove mixing some spice or other into a pot. Momma had a real talent when it came to making life in general smell good. Today, however, it didn't have the mouthwatering kick it usually did. Momma hadn't done anything different, so that means it was probably me. Maybe it was the fact that I hadn't been sleeping right, but it seemed that ever since Mr. Freeman had told me about them stars the world was a little more grey.

"Lunch will be ready in a minute," she said. "Don't you go snacking or else you'll ruin your appetite."

"I'm not really hungry," I said. I hadn't been for quite some time.

Momma abandoned her cooking and pressed her hand against my forehead. "Boy, you look like you been ridden hard and put away wet. There'll be no outside for you today. After lunch you're going straight to bed."

I grumbled a bit, but I was more going through the motions. We both had our parts to play.

"No, I won't hear it," she said. "You ain't no good unless you're well."

She and I both knew what she was referring to. That was a good a segue as any. "Momma, what's behind the skymercials?"

Her stirring slowed. "Why would you think there was anything at all?"

"That old man, Mr. Freeman, he told me there were these things called 'stars' and that they're why he doesn't like looking at the skymercials."

"God dammit!" Momma realized what she'd said and crossed herself quick. "How many times have I told you not to speak to that man?"

"But I just wanted to know."

"No! Mr. Freeman is a degenerate, a fool, and a liar. You went behind my back and spoke to him when I told you not to. Present yourself for a beating, boy."

I made a break for the door, but Momma beat me to it. She was so fast and strong back then. She grabbed my arm and dragged me to the bed, laying my bottom bare. "You. Will. Never. Go. Behind. My. Back. Again." She punctuated each word with a loud slap. "Do you hear me?"

"Yes, Momma!" She let me go. I stood and tried to pull my pants up without letting them touch my stinging butt. It didn't work so well.

"Good. Very good." Momma panted heavily. A few beads of sweat dotted her forehead. She took a deep breath. "There's nothing behind the skymercials. That's all there is. Mr. Freeman lied to you, understand?"

I nodded.

"Go wash up, and don't speak of this again."

#

The next afternoon I rose well before Momma. She wouldn't approve of what I was about to do, but I was beginning to learn with her that it was better to ask for forgiveness than permission.

I dragged Jacob out of bed to our usual hiding place. He rubbed the nuggets from his eyes. "What's this all about?" he asked. "What do you want?"

"Want? It's not I want," I said, "it's what's left to do. We've got obligations. Responsibilities."

"There you go with the funny words again."

"It's Mr. Freeman, you dink. We've got unfinished business."

"But you said so yourself: he's innocent."

My head pounded. Everything Jacob said seemed to piss me off. I took a deep breath and tried to calm down. "He might very well be—if his story checks out—but, as knights, we have a duty to follow through and investigate his claims. We need to go on a quest."

"To fetch what?"

I wrapped my arm around his shoulder and turned him towards the horizon. In the distance, a great line of mountains rose and fell like the teeth of a saw. "The truth, buddy. We go to fetch the truth."

#

The wind pressed against me with a frigid hand. I had to lean forward lest it blow me back. It was biting and fierce, tearing through my pitiful jacket like it weren't even there. I'd never experienced cold before, not on this scale anyway, and more than once I suppressed the shameful thought of turning back.

Jacob, however, was not so resolute. "My mom's gonna be real mad when she finds where I been," he said through chattering teeth. "I don't think this was such a good idea."

"Don't be dumb," I said.

"Nah, man. It's cold. Let's go back and try again tomorrow."

"There ain't ever gonna be a tomorrow! There never is. Don't you get it? Every day is the same." My feet felt numb. I quit shivering.

Jacob stopped, a stunned look freezing his face. "What are you talking about?"

"I don't know!" Tears burned my eyes. I took a deep breath and tried to force words over the lump in my throat. "There's something wrong, though. Something's wrong with this whole damned placed, and I'm terrified that if I find out what it is then I'll lose something I can never get back."

"Then why keep going?" Jacob asked.

"Because as scared as I am of losing whatever it is, I'm more scared that nothing will ever change." My chest heaved. I turned and started up the mountain once more. "Come on. The sooner we reach the top the sooner we can go home."

"No. I'm done. You should stop too." Jacob squared his shoulders and dug his heels in. He eyed me with a flinty look.

"Knights don't give up," I said.

"I s'pose they don't." Jacob started down the mountain.

"Coward!" I yelled. "Yellow-bellied chicken!" But he didn't turn. I hurled the worst of the worst at him-- for some reason I thought it might just be less painful if he'd hit me-- but Jacob didn't give me any indication he'd heard. I watched him go until he was but a pinpoint at the base of the mountain.

The wind felt so much colder now.

#

Gravel crunched beneath my feet. Up here, the trees had become scarce, shrinking to little more than shrubbery clinging to naked boulders. They looked so lonely without their carpets of grass to keep them company, or maybe they were the grass and the trees had long since gone. It was getting hard to tell.

Either way, I could certainly empathize with the trees for not wanting to be in a place like this. There weren't no sun to warm 'em. I mean, there was a sun, but despite its harsh brilliance it felt weak. It was kind of like somebody showing up for their last few days of work. They were there, but so what?

A small bush clung to an outcropping providing shelter from the wind. "I'll rest here," I muttered, leaning against its rock. My voice sounded foreign—like it belonged to somebody else—and when I spoke I felt less alone.

My week of no sleep was really hitting now.

Our camp seemed so small pressed against the side of the mountain. It was just a handful of huts blackened by roaming specs. Even the Liberty Store was tiny. Just for fun, I placed the entire camp between my thumb and forefinger. "Squish," I said, pressing my fingers together. "Squish." My eyes grew heavy. "Just a few minutes. I'll sleep for just a few minutes."

For some reason, I wasn't cold.

#

The pain felt like knives buried beneath my flesh and turned outwards. A thousand prickling points, each stabbing meat and muscles I never knew I had. I screamed, writhing, my eyes snapping open, but an arm pinned me to the ground.

"Easy. Don't go doing anything stupid now," the arm said. Mr. Freeman's yellow eyes drew into focus. "What the hell possessed you come up here?"

"I wanted to see the--"

"Shutup. Climbing a mountain like Paul Fucking Bunyan. When your mother finds out where you been she's gonna flay me standing." Mr. Freeman picked up a stick and poked at the fire he'd built against the overhang. It grew a little brighter. "You're lucky Jacob got me. You'd be dead, otherwise."

"Jacob got you?" I curled my knees to my chest. Somehow that knowledge made the pain even worse. I struggled and failed to hold back a sob. "He must think I'm real piece of work."

Mr. Freeman tapped a bottle against my head. "Drink up. It'll make it easier."

The wine tasted like the fetid scrapings off a midget's ass. It helped, though. A comfortable warmth settled into my belly as the pain receded. I handed the bottle back to him. Mr. Freeman put it to the side untouched. His hands were shaking a bit.

"I just couldn't stop thinking about them stars," I said. "It was like one of them jingles that gets in your head, y'know? It just wouldn't go away. Now I've gone and said all those horrible words."

Mr. Freeman nodded slowly. "We all get hung up on things sometimes. At least you chose something worth getting hung up on." He rubbed gently between my shoulders. "For what it's worth, I don't think Jacob is the type to hold grudges. You still best make your apologies, though."

That made me feel a bit better. Everything still hurt, though. "I sure would've liked to see 'em. The stars, I mean."

He smiled big and yellow. "Look up, boy."

And there they were; jewels sewn into a silk sky. They shimmered in the weave, drawing me from one light to the next with little pause between. Though, it wasn't the stars that held me with such fervor, but the spaces between, for in them I cast my hopes, my fears, and my most fantastic imaginings. I wove threads between the gems, creating stories and characters to match. To me, in that instant, they were more real than any experience had ever been or would be.

A couple of them kinda looked like a fish, if I squinted.

Mr. Freeman coughed, bringing me back down to Earth. I realized I'd been sitting slack jawed. "Satisfied now?" he asked.

"Yeah," I said. "I think I am."

END

A Woman's Work
by R. J. Joseph

Jamarcus was on that crazy tip before he hit the door. I could smell it on him, underneath the sweat that drenched his dingy wife beater tee.

He clumped into the kitchen, sucking his teeth. "Hamburger again?" He slammed a plastic grocery bag of empty, stinking food containers into the sink, ignoring the clean dishes already there, waiting to be rinsed.

Ten years of marriage had taught me that the conversation could go badly, whether I answered or not. I remained silent.

"You don't hear me?"

I waited a couple of beats while my own anger leapt inside my chest. My neck prickled from the fire bubbling inside my skin.

"The whole block hears you." I turned from the sink and faced him. He needed to back off. He didn't always. Jamarcus was a handsome man, with chocolate colored skin that stretched over tight muscles and gleamed from his long day at work. I had loved him dearly once, warts and all. But I was getting tired of his shit.

He stared at me a moment and threw himself into a chair like a petulant child. "I work hard, you know. I'm sick of eating the same old thing every night."

"It's the best I can do, Jamarcus, when you spend money we don't have on that bike of yours." I placed a plate with the hamburger meat and macaroni in front of him.

"Oh, I'm *gonna* get my bike tricked out. And you nagging won't stop me from going to Bike Week next month, either."

"Do I ever nag you, Jamarcus? You do whatever you want all the time and I don't say a word." He wouldn't meet my eyes, and mumbled under his breath instead.

I held myself in check long enough to gently set a glass of ice on the table next to him, along with a pitcher of fruit punch. A roach scurried underneath my feet as I walked down the hall towards the children's room.

The furious tears I'd held at bay slipped down my face as I ran my hand along our oldest son's cheek. He'd been running a fever earlier, and I was thankful he felt cooler. I didn't know where the money would have come from if I'd have had to take him to the urgent care clinic. Jamarcus would have told me the boy was alright, and to not baby them so much. But I knew when they were really sick, and Jr. was fighting some kind of kid cooties.

I kissed the three of them and replaced kicked off covers. Jamarcus would be done wolfing down his food soon, so I hurried into our bedroom. I swept the massager and warm oil from the nightstand into the wastebasket against the foot of the bed. There would be no romantic massage that evening, and I felt stupid for having thought I could salvage anything in the marriage.

There hadn't been a romantic moment between us for a very long time. I pulled off my clothes and put on the homeliest pajamas I owned, hoping to fend him off that night. He was most in the mood for the rough, quick sex that had become our staple coupling whenever he was in a foul mood. I wasn't feeling it, and I didn't want to have to fight. I made my retreat to the hall bathroom, to wait him out.

I heard him banging around in the kitchen, throwing the chair against the table. Then, I was immersed in darkness. I'd hoped the light company would give us a reprieve, since it had gotten so late in the evening and they hadn't cut our electricity yet. They must have been working late that night—there would be no rescue.

"Dammit! You didn't pay the light bill, Sasha?" I could hear more banging around. The boys slept with small battery operated fans in their room, so I didn't worry about them waking up in the heat and noise.

Even in the dark, Jamarcus found his vodka. I could almost hear him taking long swallows straight from the bottle. I leaned against the tank of the toilet, and hoped the roaches wouldn't rush out into the darkness until I'd already made it into bed. I pulled a candle out of the space saver above me and waited to light it.

After about twenty minutes, Jamarcus bustled his way to our room and threw himself down onto our bed. Nightly showering had also left his routine. I was glad I hadn't changed the sheets. He could sleep in his own funk.

Once I was sure he'd fallen asleep, I lit the candle and placed it on top of the shelf, so my babies could find their way to the bathroom during the night if they needed to.

I checked on the boys one last time, and went to the hall closet and pulled down a blanket. I made sure it was one big enough to wrap my body in completely. Despite the heat, I'd be fine as long as Jamarcus couldn't touch me. Fighting his way through the blanket would be too much work for him, so I was pretty sure I'd be safe from his stick and jab that night.

I needed a good night sleep: I had to go see Shorty the next day.

#

"Hey, Sexy. It's about time you hollered at your boy." Shorty unfolded his six feet, seven inches of caramel from behind his desk and met me halfway across the room. He nodded at the dude who'd ushered me in, and the door was closed behind him.

He pressed full lips to my cheek, and then to my lips. I allowed him to hold onto my waist for a few moments longer than I probably should have, and then pulled away.

"Hey, Shorty." I'd planned exactly what I would say to my ex-lover, but the words escaped me. But he knew me well.

"That fool acting up again?" The long lashes framing his eyes made them softer than I knew they were. I was the only person alive who knew what the gleam underneath those curtains meant. Anyone else who'd figured it out had done so too late.

I turned away from Shorty. "That's my husband. And my babies' daddy."

"Yeah, yeah. You all in love and shit." He pulled my chin back towards him with his finger. "But you're sad. Just say the word. I'll do his punk ass myself."

"It ain't like that, Shorty. Really." I still couldn't look him in the eyes. Jamarcus had lost his damned mind in the past couple of years, but I didn't want him iced. "I need some paper. Kinda short nowadays."

Shorty took one more squeeze of my waist and headed back to his desk. "I knew that poser wasn't handling his business." He slid out a drawer and pulled out stacks of cash. "How much you need, Sexy?"

I shifted my weight to the other side. "You know I'm not gonna just take money from you like that. I want to work for it. You got something or somebody for me to do?"

A different gleam shone from Shorty's eyes. "You mean like in the old days when you was on the streets for me?" He shook his head. "Um, um, um. You always were my best piece." He dropped the money and leaned on the desk.

"We were always so good together, Baby. Why won't you just come on back to Daddy?"

I sighed. "We were good. But we were also dangerous." I remembered my time with Shorty. So did my body. Heat rose from between my thighs and I could smell my arousal. Shorty could too.

He closed his eyes and inhaled deeply. He stood as if to come back to where I was and I willed him to stop. I wasn't strong enough to resist him for long.

Finally, he sighed and sat down. "Go see this dude, Hakeem. He wants in and does pretty well, but I don't know yet if I can trust him. Break him down and give him a taste." He smiled. "Just let me know where his head is at. You wearing the leather?"

"You know it. Can't tell no lies when the garters are sliding across both sides of their heads."

Shorty scribbled an address on a slip of paper and brought it to me, sliding it down between my breasts. "I'll pay you four g's when you get back." He pressed a kiss to my right breast. "And if you come back early, I'll give you a bonus."

I backed away from him towards the door. My heart pounded, not just from his kiss, but from the excitement of finally being back in the game. I knew Shorty would come through for me and I wanted to get him what he asked for. I was so glad I had avoided Jamarcus's sex the night before. I couldn't be distracted from this job with him on my skin. My baby needed to go to the doctor. Damn, I needed my lights turned back on, too.

\#

"Shorty sent me to you, like a present, you know?" I pressed myself against the bulge in Hakeem's jeans.

He waved his boys away from the room. I straddled him on the table he leaned against, and eased him down onto it.

"No shit? That mean I'm in?"

I swirled my tongue in his mouth before answering. "That depends on how you perform for me." I slid my skirt up above my hips and placed my thighs on each side of his head.

His cell phone rang, and he reached for it from his pocket, never taking his eyes off my thong clad mound.

"Yo, D, let me hit you back, man." He didn't wait for the caller to agree. The two seconds were all I'd needed to see who was on the phone.

"How you gonna answer your phone when you got all this booty in your face?" I slid my body down and dragged his arms up above his head and pinned him to the table. "That's rude."

He opened his mouth to protest, half smiling. I thrust my tongue into his mouth and coaxed his out to play. My fingernails lengthened into claws, and when his eyes shot open, I bit off his tongue.

My longer tongue slid from my nether lips and tore through the filmy leather of my panties. It wove its way through his jeans and entered his body. I lapped up his pain from his mouth, and held his legs in place with my extended, scaled toes. In my exuberance to be working again after so many years, I drank more than I should have, and I couldn't resist a few more bites than were necessary to finish him off.

Instead of taking the front door back out, I slid out the window that faced the back alley, affording myself a few more moments to savor my meal and pull myself back together.

Shorty had left by the time I returned to his office, but his boy handed me a fat envelope. I read the note. "I knew he was fucking off my money and trying to play me. Your bonus is inside, too."

I rubbed my hands across the stack and headed to the electric company offices.

#

"The fuck you been, dressed like that?" I hadn't known Jamarcus would be home early. He'd beat the kids home from school.

"I had to go pay the light bill." I moved to get past him to go change clothes, but he blocked my way.

"Where'd you get the money?"

"I borrowed it." I tried again to move around him.

"Like hell you did. You been tricking all this time, while I've been working my ass off for you?"

I felt the familiar anger bubbling again. "You don't work for me, you work for you."

He grabbed my arm and threw me against the wall. He punched me in the stomach. Recent years had escalated the violence, but he'd never outright punched me like that before. He fumbled with his belt and the realization that he was aroused tore through me.

Pain clouded my vision and I could no longer remember that I loved him or that he was the father of my children. He hiked my skirt up and entered my body.

Instead of an opening, he was met with my own appendage. It swirled around him and slid into his penis. I jerked away from him and stabbed at him with the claws I hadn't felt slide out. My sharpened teeth slurred my words.

"I'm sick of your shit." I raked down his torso in one slash and pulled my tongue from his body and tightened it around his neck.

"I fix your fuck ups and I do without because of your selfishness. My babies don't have because you're such a dick." His face ballooned with pressure.

I wanted to feed on him, but his blood was sour, his flesh rancid. I left him with his blackness.

#

I called Shorty and he came to the house for me. He held me while I cried and his boys took care of what was left of Jamarcus.

"I lost control, Shorty. I've always been able to contain myself." I sobbed.

He caressed the scales on my back and brought my head up for a kiss. "It's okay, Baby. His days were numbered. Don't know how you kept from icing his punk ass this long."

"What do I tell the boys?"

"You tell them they got a new daddy who's gonna take care of them and raise them to be real men. Y'all are coming home with me." He stroked my tongue and kissed it, too.

"He wasn't even worth eating." I spat out the residue of my ex-husband and I felt my claws begin to retract.

"I got another job for you. We go in the back door on this one, so we can go just like this."

END

Trail of Stars
by Laura Hardgrave

Hatch stared down at the flimsy piece of rusted metal and wondered what had possessed Ly to name her after a piece of graveyard junk. She kicked the warship's hatch in question. The rust disintegrated under her boot. "No good," she muttered, moving on to the next heap of metal.

The duo dusty moons of Quoi loomed over the starship junkyard, casting eerie rust-colored shadows on the ground below Hatch's feet. Despite the shadows, it was a good night for junk collecting. Visibility was decent.

"Find anything yet?" Ly asked, circling the other side of Hatch's piles. His pack was overflowing with a stack of blackened engine coils, and the grease covering them coated his leather duster. His hands were covered in splotches of black. He shot her a grin, and Hatch noticed he even had a streak of dark grease on his brown, age-etched forehead.

She shook her head, chuckling. "Those coils are a nice find. Did you really have to go swimming with them?"

"They were a little buried." He shrugged. "I found some paint too. Been a good night."

"I can see that. Looks like you managed to keep your sexy locks clean," she noted, glancing at Ly's thick waves of black hair that fell halfway down his back.

"One of us needs pretty hair."

Hatch grinned. "Leave my hair alone. I like it." She wore it cropped as short as she could, almost like a buzz cut. All long hair did was end up frizzy and get in the way.

Just then, they heard the sound of a shuttle roaring to the planet's surface behind them. "Oy," Ly muttered, "we gotta get off this hunk of junk." He leaped over the pile of metal rubbish that was between him and Hatch, grabbing her hand. "Let's fly."

Hatch's gaze ping-ponged around the junkyard. "Maybe it's not the police."

"Yeah, right. The police drones are slow. Be thankful it's them." Ly kept his eyes ahead as they began sprinting toward Wildfire, their spacecraft.

As they ran, Hatch saw the glaring spotlight of the police drones from the corner of an eye. She stumbled on a broken propeller and caught herself.

"Don't look back," Ly said. "We got time. We could do cartwheels and still outrun 'em." They could barely make out the dim silhouette of Wildfire where she was hidden beneath a large dumpster. Wildfire looked like she belonged in the junkyard herself. She meant everything to Ly--almost as much as their freedom.

Hatch heard the sick, grating whir of a police drone. She risked another frantic glance and saw the drone gaining on them. *It's too close.*

Hovering a foot above the ground, it looked like a potbellied trash can with cobalt eyes that shone in the darkness. Never blinking, never tiring of the chase. Large arms extended from a metallic torso, ready to grab its victim or destroy whatever lay in the path toward that victim--whichever came first.

The drone shone with a metallic sheen Hatch didn't recognize. Its hover pads whirred louder than she remembered. "It's closing in!" she shouted.

"Dammit!" Ly shouted between gasps for air. His dark gaze flicked toward Hatch for an instant.

A tremor ran down Hatch's spine. *Lyle Kinn is never afraid.*

Ly released her hand and leaped ahead of Hatch and over a pile of melted tires in two long-legged strides, as if he heard her terrified thought and had to prove it wrong. He wrestled with a nearby stack of black plastic wrapping, tossing quick glances back and forth from the material to the approaching drone.

"Hatch, keep going!" he called out.

She gave him a frantic gaze, but followed his cue. She leapt over the tires and sprinted toward Wildfire. She kept her head low, her body streamlined. Her slender arms and legs pumped mechanically, covered in the sheen of sweat. Growing up under the wing of a ship graveyard smuggler had its benefits--namely, adapting to life on the run.

She slammed the button on her comm belt that opened Wildfire's hatch. As she propelled herself toward the slow-rising door, the cold arm of a drone swept against her shoulder. She ducked low to the ground and fell into a body roll that carried her up the ship's ramp and inside the entryway. Her shoulder hit the corner of the ramp, and tendrils of pain shot through her shoulder and arm. As she winced and recovered from the roll, Hatch caught a glimpse of Ly bolting out from behind a dumpster, covering the drone in plastic.

"Start 'er up, Hatch!" he shouted. His lanky body clung to the top of the drone as the machine bucked Ly around like a wild horse. The drone's vision sensors were temporarily disabled from the obstruction, and

it flailed its appendages around haphaz-
ardly, trying to grab hold of Ly.

Hatch knew she didn't have much time.
Once the drone caught hold of Ly, he'd never
survive the fight. She slammed Wildfire's
door shut, raced toward the cockpit, and
started the liftoff sequence. "Duke, drop a
line for Ly!" she shouted.

A three-foot tall decrepit-looking robot
appeared from the ship's cabin and raised a
single shutter-eyebrow at Hatch. "He is getting far too old for this," the robot noted as
he rotated his wheels and headed to the rear
of the ship.

Duke was treated more like a member of
the oddball family than the hunk of metal he
really was. Ly had built Duke up from an old
AI core and spare parts he found at junk-
yards through the years. "Ready," Duke said,
after hitting a few switches.

Wildfire roared to life under Hatch's controls and rose up in the air, illuminating the night with a hazy orange glare. Her rear porthole popped open, and Hatch navigated the ship over Ly's location where he was locked in death's grip with the plastic-covered drone. A rope ladder uncoiled above his head.

Hatch flipped on the outside comm, and shouted out to Ly. "Grab the ladder!"

Ly gave the drone one last heave and leaped off its back and onto the ladder. When Hatch saw he was starting to climb, she piloted Wildfire up into the air, leaving behind the flailing drone and its quickly-incoming companions.

Ly appeared from the rear of the cabin with an exhausted grin plastered to his face. His face and hair were covered in sweat. "Whew!" he said. "That was one hell of an escape!"

Duke's metallic-tinged voice sounded from the rear of the cabin as he closed and secured the porthole. "You sure about that, master? You have one of those escapes, what, every few days?"

The robot's voice chip was advanced enough so he didn't sound like the old dinosaur models from the past, but his tone was still noticeably mechanical. His voice chip also boosted a modern, adaptive vocabulary. When Ly found Duke's voice chip, he'd had a lucky night.

"Nah, nothing quite close to *that* chase scene," Ly said, tossing Duke an excited nod. "Those drones came outta nowhere. Must be a new model." He dropped his bag of greasy coils that had somehow survived his wrestling match to the ship's floor.

"Think so?" Hatch asked as she rose Wildfire up to the lower levels of Quoi's atmosphere. She still hadn't sat down in her co-pilot's seat. She knelt over the ship's control panel, her knees caught in tight locks. Her heart wouldn't stop tumbling over itself inside her chest, and she was afraid that if she bent her knees, she'd slide right to the floor.

Ly glanced out of a side window, watching the rusted surface of Quoi disappear. "Yeah. I've never seen them come after us that fast." He wiped the sweat from his face with a sleeve as his grin dissolved. "You okay, Hatch?"

She nodded without facing him. "Bit shaken up. I'll be okay."

He approached her from behind and placed a hand on her shoulder. "We'll be okay," he said softly. "I'm sorry. It made me kinda nervous too, I have to admit."

Hatch winced as his hand tightened on her shoulder.

"Shit," Ly said, removing his hand. "Did it get you by the door?"

She shrugged. "I think so. Nothing major."

"Here, let me take her," Ly said as he grabbed Wildfire's main controls from beneath Hatch. "Take off your jacket. Duke, grab the med kit."

"Nah, it's no--"

"--No, it's *not* nothing," Ly interrupted. "Let us see."

Hatch sighed and slid off her leather jacket. Beneath it, she wore a white tank top. A patch of dark skin dangled from a purple bruise where she had collided with Wildfire's frame. "It looks like it ripped my jacket too." She shrugged again, then took a moment to wipe some of the sweat off her brow.

"Shit," Ly said, grimacing. That's gonna be painful as it heals."

One of Duke's skinny metal sticks that served as an arm shoved a tube of ointment into her face. "This will ease the swelling and pain."

"Ly, shut up," she said, shoving her way past the two of them. "It's not even bleeding anymore. I'm gonna take a shower after we get out of orbit. That's all I need. Duke, take the cockpit with Ly." She sat down on one of the narrow passenger seats and strapped herself in.

Ly tossed her another worried glance, but obliged, taking a seat in the captain's chair. Duke extended the rods above his wheels and secured himself to the seat next to him. After strapping themselves in, Wildfire's hyperdrive thrusters powered on, and after a moment of rattling and shaking, the ship roared into space.

Hatch stared stubbornly out of the tiny passenger window as they made their ascent. She watched the stars blur as they flashed by like an ancient kaleidoscope. Her shoulder throbbed, but what worried her more were the images in her mind of the police drone racing toward her, its claw-tipped appendages flailing inches below Ly's heart. *Too damned close of a call.*

The stars outside Wildfire's window shimmered back into reality as the ship's hyperspace thrusters cut out again. Duke unfastened himself from the co-pilot's chair and rolled over to Ly's pack. He rummaged through it while Hatch kept her eyes focused on the dark window.

"Paint, master?" Duke asked.

"Yeah, for you!" Ly said. "We're gonna finally get rid of your greys and browns and rust-flecks. Make you all one color."

Turning away from the window, Hatch couldn't resist a smile.

Duke's coiled eyes widened. "I'm so glad! Paint's a rare find."

"Nothing's too rare for my Duke." Ly unclicked his safety belt and approached Hatch. He grabbed the tube of ointment where Duke had left it and handed it to her. "Here, clean up your shoulder. I need to change before I cover the whole ship in this gunk that's--"

Ly collapsed to the ship's grated floor before he could finish his sentence. Duke rolled over to him and Hatch bolted up from her seat.

"Ly, dammit!" Hatch said. "Don't tell me you got hurt and didn't feel it again!" Two years ago, Ly had broken a rib during a standoff with a planetary thug over a piece of transport motor. He failed to mention the injury until Hatch found him doubled over inside his bunk.

"Hey, I really thought that was... nothing," Ly managed through gritted teeth. He clutched his left thigh.

"You need to find a safer day job, master," Duke said.

"My turn to try and talk sense into you," Hatch said. "Let me see." She knelt down beside Ly and removed his clenched hand. A dark stain pooled beneath the fabric of his jeans. "You're bleeding! Take off your pants."

"Hey now... that's fool talk unless there's a pretty lady nearby."

A drop of sweat from Ly's forehead landed on Hatch's arm, and she glared at him. "Now's really not the time."

Ly grimaced and unbuckled his pants. Hatch slid them off, leaving him in his boxers. A black gash revealed itself, seeping blood that seemed as dark as the grease that coated Ly's coat.

"Master, did the drone's claw appendage do this?" Duke asked.

"I don't... Maybe." Ly clenched his eyes shut as Hatch grabbed some gauze and applied pressure to the wound. "Shit! That hurts, Hatch!"

"Yeah, yeah. It's supposed to. Why the hell is this blood so dark?" Hatch stared open-mouthed at Ly as dark blood seeped through the layers of gauze.

"It doesn't look natural," Duke agreed. "You said the drones belonged to a new build?"

"They had to... have been," Ly said, his voice forced. His sweat-glistened face paled as Hatch kept pressure on the gauze. "Why's it so... painful?"

"I don't know, master. But it's possible that if the drones were made of a new alloy material, the metal may have left toxins in your body. They could be specifically designed that way, in order to--"

"We gotta get you to an emergency station!" Hatch interrupted.

"We... can't." Ly groaned through gritted teeth.

"Master's right. We have a cargo hold full of illegal AI chips for delivery. There's no way we'd get through station security."

"It's an emergency. They have to let us through."

"No, they don't. The government could care less about smuggler ships like ours."

"What are we supposed to do then?" Hatch looked between Ly's ashen and Duke's stoic faces.

"Wait it out... just like every other complication we've encountered," Ly said.

"Complication? We're gonna wait out *poison*? And what if it kills you?" Hatch added another hunk of gauze to her pile and met Ly's gaze, challenging him.

Duke's eye-shutters widened. "Master. There is that doctor on Juko. We delivered illegal drugs to her seven months ago. She lost the funding for her refugee clinic, so she gave us some stolen arms to sell in return."

"Oh... right," Ly said, remembering. "She was cute. Though I think she... had eyes for Hatch, not me." He made an attempt to laugh, but his eyes clamped shut again. He groaned instead.

"Shut up and quit trying to move," Hatch grumbled. "Duke, set a course for Juko. I'm gonna give you pain meds and try to suction out some of the poison."

Ly opened an eye and winced. "I knew I should have... dropped you off at med school instead of keeping you locked up here. Spinning around the... galaxy."

"What did I say about shutting up?" Hatch shook her head and rummaged through the med kit. She'd never been much of a bookworm, but a cool head and lack of squeamishness went a long way when it came to sharing a ship with a crazy smuggler like Ly.

"Yes, ma'am. I mean... mom... Boy, I'm glad I'm not your real dad, or this might be... pretty damn awkward."

A smile slid onto the corners of Hatch's face as she held a large needle in front of Ly's widening eyes. "Pain meds should help with the shutting up part."

#

Four hours later, Hatch found herself inside Wildfire's tiny shower, attempting to rinse away the fear and grime that coated every pore on her body. Only one coating came clean with water. The layer of fear dusted her skin and every organ, stubborn and insistent, like the cold reaches of space that surrounded them.

Ly had finally passed out right before Hatch hopped in the shower. She had to use both bottles of painkillers to relax him in order to drain some of the poison from his blood.

The toxin was as stubborn as Hatch's dust coating, and the instant she tried to suction his blood, it coagulated, becoming thick as tar. She pulled out what clots she could with her gloved fingers, but the rest had disappeared from the wound's surface. The good news was that the bleeding had stopped. The bad news was that the poison had receded deep into his tissue.

This could be it. The thought propelled itself into her mind as the last of the soap suds disappeared down the drain. *Most would consider Ly lucky to have lived this long.*

She knew the next step was most likely cutting deep into Ly's skin, but Hatch wasn't a doctor, nor did she have the tools to try such a crazy move.

The warm water above her head shut off, signaling the end to her shower. She dried herself off, spreading some of Duke's ointment on her shoulder.

"Are you decent?"

Hatch sighed at the sound of Duke's polite voice from the other side of the restroom. "What is it?"

"We're ready to enter Juko's orbit. I will need your assistance with seeking entry."

"Got it. Be out in a couple."

Hatch entered her bunk and threw on a clean pair of jeans and a tank top. Inside her locker, she noticed a strand of hanging leather.

It was the turquoise glass and leather cord she'd had since Ly found her on the junkyard heaps of Kyrio 16 years ago. Ly hadn't known how to feed or clothe her, but he knew how to make her smile. He found a tear-shaped piece of glass and would twirl it in the light of the setting sun above Kyrio, sending bright green triangles flickering against every panel of Wildfire's hull.

Much to his pleasure, Ly found out that three-year-old Hatch was easily amused. Still was, if caught in the right mood. Smiling, she pocketed the piece of glass and joined Duke in the cockpit.

The robot gave her as best of a distraught look as he could muster. "Juko's transit station is seeking a legal dumping certificate."

"That's right--ours expired here two months ago."

"What do we do? Master will not respond."

Hatch glanced down at Ly, who was laying on their dining table, sprawled out and snoring. "There isn't time to get a new one forged. Let's see if we can sweet talk our way out of this."

"Can't we just tell them the truth?"

"Nope. Our doctor's clinic isn't exactly legal. The planet's just a dumping ground for shuttle parts and refugees. Neither of which deserve medical care according to the officials." Hatch took a seat in the captain's chair and switched on the comm link. "Juko transit patrol?"

"Copy, Wildfire. Please transmit an image of your certificate."

"That, um, might be difficult," Hatch said. "We recently had a small fire in our cockpit. Half the database panel got knocked out. We have the replacement parts onboard, but we need access to a dumping site."

"And the fire conveniently knocked out all landing certs, but not communications or flight controls?"

"Yes."

"Uh-huh. Original. Try again."

Hatch muted the comm and hung her head on Wildfire's controls. "I suck at this."

"Let me try," Duke said. He flicked on the comm again.

"My mistress is telling the truth. In fact, my master sustained an injury in the fire, and he's recovering as we speak. I can show you the... grease that caused the fire."

The two glanced down at the pile of greasy coils that hadn't budged from the cockpit's floor. Hatch shrugged at Duke. The robot apparently wasn't any better at making up stories than she was. *Dammit, Ly, why are you so good at this crap?*

"Grease? What the hell, you running a fast food joint on that dump of a ship?"

The interface below Hatch's drooped head beeped suddenly. "Hold on," she said, shutting off the comm. She clicked on the other link. The message came from Juko's surface.

"Is this Wildfire? Lyle Kinn's ship?" It was a woman.

"Yes. Who's this?" Hatch and Duke exchanged nervous glances.

"This is Dr. Amanda Cellas. Call me Amanda. I overheard your comm with transit. Your name was Hatch, right? Never forget that name. Your droid's voice gave you away."

"Oh, man. Am I glad you listened in on that. We need your help. Drones were hot on our tail, and Ly took a poisoned--"

"Hold on. That's all I need to hear. I'll send you a temp cert and the coordinates for a hidden landing site. I've had to move my clinic. I'll meet you there."

"Copy. Thank you. And... bring a transport. Ly's out cold."

Moments later, Hatch and the doctor hurried toward the refugee clinic hidden among the ruins of an old Juko factory. Ly sat slumped in a wheelchair, his face covered in a sheen of sweat.

Dr. Cellas adjusted the oxygen mask she wore and checked Ly's initial readings on her mobile scanner while Hatch pushed him. They ducked under a low, crumbling wall.

"I'd say this place is hidden," Hatch said, taking a deep breath. The air was dense and reeked of filthy smoke. "The pollution's worse than I remember."

"Half the planet was shot at with pollution nukes six months ago. It made most of the refugee camps inhabitable. These people can't afford food, let alone masks."

"Officials wanted to kill them off?"

"Seems so. Hid the whole thing under wraps. No one wants to deal with the remnants of war."

"Killing half the planet is a better option?"

"Cheaper, at least. Families join the military or succumb to bombs. Most other planets are following the example." The doctor turned back to her scanner. "Shit. This was what I was afraid of."

"What is it?"

"The new police drones are made with an upgraded alloy. Any contact below the skin sends toxin directly to the bloodstream. The toxin's a way to take care of criminals who manage to escape."

"Take... care?"

Amanda toyed with one of her tiny, black braids as she avoided Hatch's gaze. "It does one of two things--kills its victim, or disables their nerve functions entirely. For the latter, the toxin can also be used as a tracking device."

"The drones will be tracking our every move?"

"Exactly."

"Shit."

"I agree. We have a limited window. My clinic's just inside that parking garage."

They broke into a run, pushing Ly between the two of them. Dodging hunks of blackened concrete, they made their way into the rusted shack that served as Dr. Cel-las' clinic.

Once inside, Amanda led them to the back of the clinic, shoving aside her other patients. Plastic coating surrounded the walls, attempting to create a sterile field. She threw off her mask, barked a few orders to her assistant, then closed the plastic tight. "I'll have to amputate his entire leg, but I need to scan and track the toxin first. Sure you want to be in here?"

Hatch's breath caught inside her throat. It was as though the pollution from outside had settled behind her tongue, stubbornly taking cover. "Yeah."

The doctor met her gaze and nodded. She went to work beneath the bright sheen of plastic.

Hatch sat cross-legged on the floor near the operating table, head buried in her hands. For what seemed like hours, Amanda worked on Ly. A dull current of activity echoed from the other side of the plastic. Refugees entered the clinic with pollution poisoning, right after another. A child wailed. A mother screamed for food and supplies, even though the clinic didn't have access to either.

The memory of Quoi's duo moons sauntered into Hatch's numb sense of reality, and within the cries from the refugees, waves of rusted moonlight floated over piles of debris. The waves seemed to call out to Hatch, reminding her that everything touched by war disintegrated into dusty trails.

The dust threatened to choke her until a face appeared above her slumped shoulders. Amanda's.

"I did all I could," she said, her face pulled tight. "Amputated the leg below the joint, transfused as much blood as I could. Trace amounts of the toxin still coat his veins. There's nothing I can do about that, but his body might be able to fight back. We should know in a few minutes, by watching the cells." She slid down to the floor next to Hatch, rubbing her temples.

Hatch turned to her. "Thank you, Amanda. If anyone can fight this thing, it's Ly."

"I know. He's... not your father, is he? I wanted to ask last time we met. You two don't look all that much alike. Not at all, in fact."

"No," Hatch said." He found me when I was three, inside a ship graveyard. I was hidden under an old ship's hatch. Stupidly enough, it was the hatch that protected me from the storms that circled the planet. I guess he found the word fitting."

Amanda laughed. "I'd wondered. No idea who your real parents are?"

Hatch shook her head and let her gaze drift toward Ly, who now appeared to be resting comfortable under a blanket of heavy sedatives. His face was still ashen, his breathing shallow. "I used to get angry when people gave us weird stares, but it doesn't bother me anymore. Ly's been better to me than any parent."

"He doesn't strike me as the fatherly type. No offense."

"He escaped a military brat's life. Never knew much about kids. But he did what he had to. He makes life... entertaining." Hatch reached into her pocket and pulled out the tiny chunk of turquoise glass. She spun the cord between two fingers, watching the sharp edges twirl in the surgical lights.

Amanda gave her what looked like an exhausted smile, then stood up to check Ly's vitals. The smile on her face vanished.

"Dammit," Hatch mumbled. Her chest tightened. Her fist clenched the leather cord as she approached Ly's bedside. "He's not going to make it, is he?"

"I'm afraid not, Hatch. His vitals are slipping. The toxin's moving through his bloodstream again, toward his heart."

"Antibiotics?"

"The tech's too new. I promise you, that'll be the next project I work on." The doctor met Hatch's eyes with determined eyes. "His heart's failing. You should say your... goodbyes."

"Can he hear me?"

"Possibly." Amanda turned away from Hatch and Ly, giving them a moment.

Hatch clamped Ly's hand in hers, taking a deep breath. "I guess... Duke was right. We do need to find a safer day job. But I... wouldn't take back any of it. The fights. Chases.

Loved every escape route you showed me."
She gave the turquoise glass another
squeeze, then placed it back inside her
pocket.

"I'll... take care of Duke, and Wildfire,
and..." A tear slid down her cheek, and she
reached out with her other hand to stroke
Ly's long hair.

His chest rose and fell once more, then
his heart stopped.

A second tear joined Hatch's first.
"Thank you for... the spin around the galaxy," she whispered.

Turning back to Hatch, Amanda clicked
off the monitors hooked up to Ly's body. Her
voice was soft. "This is poor timing, I realize,
but I just got a message. The police squad's
on their way here. They must have tracked
the toxin."

Hatch's eyes clenched shut as she focused
on gathering her senses. Her head spun with

the memory of Ly's smile and the backdrop of stars that accompanied it. In one quick motion, her eyelids fluttered open again. "We can't let them find your clinic. Let's fly."

They placed Ly's body back in the wheelchair and exited Amanda's clinic, breaking into a run after clearing the rusted doorway. A line of grime-covered patients tossed angry shouts to the doctor as they ran.

Juko's polluted air assaulted them as they sprinted through the ruins of fallen concrete. Rust-colored dust swirled through the air.

The whir of the police drones sounded behind them, coming from the direction of the clinic.

"No!" Amanda shouted, her voice hoarse. "They found it!"

Hatch ducked behind a charred wall, dragging Ly's wheelchair and the doctor with her. A pair of police spotlights roamed the area, gulping in the war-torn air. Hatch shushed Amanda, and the two remained frozen for a few precious seconds, taking hurried breaths.

"You have to come with Duke and I," Hatch said, meeting Amanda's desperate gaze.

Shouts began to echo across the ruins as police drones inspected the refugees inside the clinic. Whether they survived the inspection or not would depend on any attempt to struggle.

Amanda opened her mouth as if to speak, then was silenced again by Hatch, who crouched down against the wall, her eyes focused on the pair of lights. "We run when that spotlight passes over us next round. No time to argue."

The light passed over, and Hatch grabbed Amanda's shaking hand and a handle of Ly's wheelchair. "Don't look back."

They ran with all their strength toward Wildfire's hiding spot. Hatch refused to look behind her this time. Instead, she slammed on the ship's comm with a free thumb. "Duke, start her up, and open the cargo hatch! We're making a quick getaway!"

Amanda shot her another terrified glance as they sprinted across the final stretch. Wildfire's taillights illuminated their path, and just as the sound of whirring drones began to thrum in Hatch's ears, the group burst into the ship's cargo hold.

"You in, mistress?" Duke asked through the comm.

"We're in. Got us a doctor. Now get us off this planet."

The robot hesitated. "And... master?"

"Ly didn't make it, Duke. I'm sorry. I brought his body onboard. I was hoping we could spread his ashes among the stars. Make a trail with 'em."

"He would like that."

The ship rumbled to life beneath their feet as Hatch and Amanda caught their breaths.

"I've never been so thankful for pure oxygen," Amanda said, wiping her brow. "Don't know how the refugees do it. Or... you smugglers."

Hatch gave her a weak smile. "It takes some getting used to. That gives me an idea. How's a mobile clinic sound, Amanda? We can smuggle on the side, you know, to pay the bills."

"Y-you... Really?" Amanda stammered.

"Sure. I'd be glad to help out. No more running from officials."

"More like... flying from them?"

Hatch fingered the shard of glass within her pocket. "Exactly. Making our own trail, in memory of the one Ly fought for."

"What trail is that?"

"Freedom.

END

www.ingramcontent.com/pod-product-compliance
Lightning Source LLC
Chambersburg PA
CBHW032240010726
47494CB00002B/565